SPIDERS' WAR

Borgo Press Books by S. Fowler Wright

Arresting Delia: An Inspector Cleveland Classic Crime Novel
The Attic Murder: An Inspector Combridge & Mr. Jellipot Classic Crime Novel
The Bell Street Murders: An Inspector Combridge & Mr. Jellipot Classic Crime Novel
Beyond the Rim: A Lost Race Fantasy
Black Widow: A Classic Crime Novel
The Capone Caper: Mr. Jellipot vs. the King of Crime: A Classic Crime Novel
Crime & Co.: An Inspector Cleveland Classic Crime Novel
Dawn: A Novel of Global Warming
Dead by Saturday: An Inspector Cleveland Classic Crime Novel
Dream; or, The Simian Maid: A Fantasy of Prehistory (Marguerite Cranleigh #1)
Elfwin: An Historical Novel
The End of the Mildew Gang: An Inspector Cauldron Classic Crime Novel (Mildew Gang #3)
Four Callers in Razor Street: An Inspector Combridge & Mr. Jellipot Classic Crime Novel
The Hanging of Constance Hillier: An Inspector Cleveland Classic Crime Novel
The Hidden Tribe: A Lost Race Fantasy
The Jordans Murder: An Inspector Combridge & Mr. Jellipot Classic Crime Novel
The King Against Anne Bickerton: A Classic Crime Novel
The Mildew Gang: An Inspector Cauldron Classic Crime Novel (Mildew Gang #1)
Murder in Bethnal Square: An Inspector Combridge & Mr. Jellipot Classic Crime Novel
The Police and the Public: Some Thoughts on the British System of Justice
Post-Mortem Evidence: An Inspector Combridge & Mr. Jellipot Classic Crime Novel
The Return of the Mildew Gang: An Inspector Cauldron Classic Crime Novel (Mildew Gang #2)
The Rissole Mystery: An Inspector Combridge & Mr. Jellipot Classic Crime Novel
The Screaming Lake: A Lost Race Fantasy
The Secret of the Screen: An Inspector Combridge & Mr. Jellipot Classic Crime Novel
Spiders' War: A Novel of the Far Future (Marguerite Cranleigh #3)
Three Witnesses: A Classic Crime Novel
Too Much for Mr. Jellipot: An Inspector Combridge & Mr. Jellipot Classic Crime Novel
The Vengeance of Gwa: A Fantasy of Prehistory (Marguerite Cranleigh #2)
Was Murder Done? A Classic Crime Novel
Who Murdered Reynard? A Classic Crime Novel
The Wills of Jane Kanwhistle: An Inspector Combridge & Mr. Jellipot Classic Crime Novel
With Cause Enough?: An Inspector Combridge & Mr. Jellipot Classic Crime Novel

SPIDERS' WAR

A NOVEL OF THE FAR FUTURE

by

S. FOWLER WRIGHT

THE BORGO PRESS

An Imprint of Wildside Press LLC

MMIX

CONTENTS

PROLOGUE

INTERVIEW WITH A MAGICIAN

"IT is a long while," the magician said, "since you were here. I had supposed that your last adventure had been enough, even for you."

Marguerite Cranleigh, who, whether the time had been long or short, looked little older than when she had bargained first for the acquaintance of distant days, gave a smiling reply: "It was exciting enough. But I cannot live in past days. I must ask you this: when I went into a far time, there was one whom I knew well. If I should go again into some distant time, could I meet him again?"

"It would not be beyond possibility."

"And could it be at a future day, rather than one which is past? You can see that I should prefer that, if it would not be beyond your power to control."

"Why should it? Between past and future there is no difference at all."

"You mean that they are equally easy for you?"

"I mean what I say. Past and present and future—they are all one. They are like the rotundity of the earth, which is not limitless, but has neither beginning nor end. You can move upon it, as I have moved you in time, but you cannot properly say that you go forward or back."

"All the same, you know what I mean."

"So I do. Some things are harder to explain than to understand."

"Then it is for that I will ask. And I should prefer a less primitive time than I had before."

"You mean a less primitive place. There have been no periods in the whole history of civilized or semi-civilized man when they have not been both orderly and savage parts of the earth, as there are today, although movement is the special development, as it must be the disintegrating factor, of the civilization to which we belong."

7

"A time when movement will be less worshiped would please me well. But there is another thing I would ask, though with little hope."

"Few things are beyond hope. What is it?"

"It is that, when I am in that far time, I may remember what I am here."

"You ask much. Have you other desires beyond that?"

"I would ask to remain, if the one of whom I speak should be there."

"So you could, while that life will last. But after that, you must return here, and find that you are in the same time as before."

"But it will not be the same, for another memory will be mine."

"You see gain in that? Well, so perhaps it may be. It is with yourselves."

"Yes. I see that."

"Even so, you may be asking more than I can certainly pledge. When you were translated before, you went into the past, and returned with memories which were easy to keep. But, if you are resolved to enter a future time, I cannot promise that you will bring back a memory of that which will not have occurred."

"But I thought you said—" she exclaimed, in some natural astonishment, and was interrupted by: "I have said too much."

He became practical, remembering the rent of the Bond Street suite in which this interview was taking place, and that the present was the only tense which its landlord would understand. He asked: "Have you brought a check?"

Yes, she had done that.

CHAPTER I.

THE ANTICIPATION OF A GOOD MEAL

SHE lay on her side. Her wrists were tied tightly behind her back. Her ankles were tied also, painfully. That was the one clear consciousness in a mind that was confused by two conflicting memories, and only dimly aware of the seated figure before her, in the gloom of the fire-lit room.

For the magician had kept his word. She could still remember that she was Marguerite Cranleigh—a memory still clear, but strangely remote. But she was Gleda now, and she could also remember the violence which that young woman had suffered in the last hour—the useless struggle against a strength far greater than hers; the binding of hands and feet; the rough tumbling into the bottom of the canoe, which, in the next moment, had been loosed from the bank, and swept down the swift current of the river toward the falls; and the sight of the strained face of the man who paddled desperately to escape a danger which, she supposed, must otherwise bear her to unavoidable death, bound as she was. (But what better had she to hope now, beyond the delay of a few hours?)

There had been the sound of the falls, louder and nearer with every stroke of the frantic paddle. And then the grating of the keel, as the canoe grounded, just as she thought that all hope had gone.

After that he had pulled her out, and flung her over his shoulder, and brought her here, for a purpose which she did not know, and could only fear—the man who was sitting before her now.

The magician surely could not have meant this—that she—Marguerite—should come here only to die in a few hours, and that in a most repugnant way, and for a use which no one would wish to serve. He must have made a mistake. Perhaps, when dealing with enormous distances of time, it was possible, even for his art, to be a few years, or a few centuries, wrong. Or a single hour might mean that the rolling earth would receive her at a widely different point.

(Or was that nonsense, or not?) Or perhaps she was to have some miraculous escape, for which her ingenuity would be enough. But that was hard to think, for she—Gleda—was now on the side of the river far from any friend. And to recross it would be, for her, an impossible thing. She would have said impossible for anyone a few hours before.

She looked at the man. He was the largest, best-made man that she (as Gleda) had ever seen. Now he wrote as though he had no other interest on his mind; a student rather than the man of action that she had seen him to be, to her own cost. He wrote as one who works against time, as, in fact, he did.

He wrote from right to left, using his left hand, which did not seem strange to her, though her dual memories conflicted. Would the old memory become weaker, and the newly acquired one stronger, as the days passed? That seemed likely enough, but then, what days would there be? The consciousness of present peril, dimmed at intervals by the strangeness, the unreality, of the whole event, became acute. If there had been no mistake, and if she were to make no nearer acquaintance with the black caldron which stood by the great kitchen fireplace which could be seen through the half-opened door, she must exert her ingenuity to avert her impending fate. Could she break her bonds? It seemed hopeless to try as they now were. Could she induce him to ease them? Anything may be asked. She said: "The ropes are too tight. They are cutting my flesh."

He looked up. Speech was different on her side of the river, but not so much so that he failed to understand. She met eyes that were not hostile, but unconcerned. He said: "You must be safely tied. I do not mean you to wriggle free. If I should have to catch you again, you might get more hurt than you are now. You will not feel it for long. You must find comfort in that."

"It is no consolation at all. Could I not be of better use?"

"Not for us. We need food. Would I have risked so much for anything else?"

It was to continue the conversation, rather than from any acute discomfort in the fire-warmed room, that she went on: "I am cold, being uncovered. Is there any profit in that?"

The man did not answer, but he got up, showing a tall and muscular form. He wore a fur cloak, loose from his shoulders, open in front. He had no other garment at all. At need, he could draw it closely, fastening it with thongs.

Seeing his height and girth, she understood how he had been able to cross the great river below the peninsula without being car-

10

ried over the falls, which she had been taught to regard as beyond human capacity. From the point where the two rivers joined, there was no more than a half a mile of swift, smooth water. He had crossed it by launching his canoe at the highest possible point, and had been carried down the very verge of the falls before he could reach the opposite shore.

Then he had carried the canoe as far as would be of any avail up the opposite bank, lain in wait for one he could capture without rousing alarm, and had been fortunate enough (as he saw it) to get someone who was young and well-fed.

It had been a bold adventure, with extreme perils, both from the flood and from human foes. Yet his face was rather that of one who thought than of one who lived by physical deeds. Now it had no expression at all, as he took down a fur cloak from a wooden peg and threw it over her with a careless but accurate cast.

She saw that furs were everywhere. They hung on the walls. They made soft coverings for the floor. On her side of the river, this would be a certain sign that he was a man of high rank.

She might have said more, but at that moment a woman entered the room. She was young and well, though rather heavily formed, yet with the gauntness that came from some weeks of scanty feeding.

She had a blunt-featured, unattractive face—particularly so to Gleda, as she licked her lips, and said: "What is the catch like?" adding: "I've not had a real bite since yesterday."

"You can judge that for yourself," he said, and already she had twitched off the fur, and was looking down on the bound form with greedy anticipation, hard to be endured.

She knelt down for closer examination, prodding here and there. She said, grunting with satisfaction: "She should be fit for the knife now. There's some meat there!"

She stood up, and walked round to her victim's back, pushing her toes into a well-shaped buttock. She said: "We owe Relf a ham. I suppose we must send it back. It's a better one than we had from him."

"Yes," the man replied. "I dislike a debt. I shall be glad for it to be cleared."

The woman left the room, followed by Gleda's warmest hatred.

Gleda said: "I should make a better wife for you than she."

The man gave her a glance which seemed both speculative and amused. He said "Well, so you might," but did not appear to regard the proposition seriously, and the woman was back before the idea could be developed further.

11

She came with a burden of wooden logs, which she piled on the fire. She asked: "You have all you need in the pen?"

He rose, saying: "I am not sure. Shall we go see?"

She looked surprised, and made no motion to follow him as he moved toward the door. She said, while he opened it, and the light of the setting sun shone inward, relieving the gloom of the low-ceiled room: "You don't need me out there."

"Yes. Come on. There may be things to arrange."

She looked puzzled, but followed, being eager in her hunger that the details of slaughtering should not be delayed.

Gleda was left alone in the stillness of the fire-lit room. The shadows leaped on the walls. There was noise and a scatter of sparks when a log fell, but she was unconscious of that. Her mind was on the terror of what must be in the next hour. Fundamental customs were the same on both banks of the river, on neither of which was cannibalism a frequent practice, as indeed, for economic reasons, it never has been in the history of the human race, Supplies would fail. But if an enemy, a criminal, or a lunatic, had to be destroyed, who would waste good meat? There would be plain folly in that.

But now there must be a condition of abnormal famine, of which she had not been aware, so completely did the river separate communication. It was a division which had also secured her people from the same privations, for the epidemic which had destroyed the swine had not crossed the barrier of the flood.

Here was a civilization at once high and simple. Sources of food were few, but they had been normally reliable, and involved little toil. In the summer men fed largely on nuts and fruits, which the forests gave. During winter, which was sharp, though short, they relied mainly on stores of nuts, which would have been gathered on warmer days. And through all the year they had ample supplies of flesh from a species of swine, herding in half-wild condition in the great woods, which spread far in a level land. There were many clearings sufficient for the spacious wooden houses of a large population, but, instead of their being surrounded by wide open spaces of arable or pasture land, here which bore many varieties of nuts and fruits, edible in their seasons, or fit to be stored for the winter months. And, if they fell ungathered—well, there were the fattening swine below that would avert waste.

The trees gave abundant material for building. They provided fuel and food. Some of them supplied a thread from which strong cloth could be woven. Here was a civilization which had become simple and self-sufficient; which had rejected the worship of mechanical power, that had brought its predecessors to servitude and then to destruction. Almost the only trade was with distant hillmen, who sold them furs in exchange for the food which they had always been able to spare abundantly. To use these skins was the privilege of the only aristocracy—an aristocracy of intellect—which their social order recognised or required. And the right to these skins was the only privilege which that aristocracy had. It had no power—unless that of persuasion—at all.

But now calamity had come. A fatal infectious disease was destroying their herds of swine in such great numbers it seemed that in a few further weeks there would be nothing left to destroy. It had followed months of drought, which were over now, and there was fresh green in the rain-drenched woods. But damage had been done which was quite as serious as the fever that killed the swine. For the nuts had fallen before they filled.

Loss of the nut crop would not have meant absolute famine, nor would loss of swine—but the two at once were bringing starvation upon the land.

Left alone, Gleda began a desperate, futile effort to loosen her bonds. She caused herself some additional pain, but otherwise did nothing, and it was only for a few brief moments that she had strained and wriggled when she was startled by a shrill and surprising sound.

CHAPTER II.

SLAUGHTER!

THE man led the way to a low-walled sty, where it was customary to confine captured swine, until they were slaughtered there. It was thickly strewn with a species of dried grass.

The woman asked: "What do you want me to do?"

"You might give the stone a turn."

She protested rather than asked, "Couldn't you have done that?"

So he could. It was not a large stone. Such stones in that land were precious and few. But she gave it a few turns while he pressed the blade of a knife against it, which, she thought, was sufficiently sharp already.

Then he said: "That will do. But we'd better leave her a few hours yet," to which the woman gave a grunt of unwilling assent. She added: "There's nothing more to be done here?"

"No," he said. "Except this."

She had turned to go out of the sty, and he was immediately behind her. As he spoke, his left arm came round her, under her breasts, and his right, holding the knife, rather lower down. The point touched her navel, and he drove it in upward with a firm thrust.

As he pulled it out, she gave the shrill scream which Gleda had heard, and which caused her to pause in her useless wriggling.

The man's arm loosed her, and she stumbled forward, her hands pressing her belly in the vain, instinctive effort to hold back the spurting blood.

The man watched her for a moment, but there was no use in standing there. Everything which was necessary had been done. He went in.

Gleda saw him coming toward her, with the knife, which he had wiped on the grass, still in his hand. She gave so desperate a struggle that she actually felt her ankles loosen, at which he smiled.

He said: "I can do better than that." He bent over her and cut the cords. "You said you could make a good wife?"

She answered, with a sudden bewildered hope: "I could try."

"Then get on your feet. You'll be able to walk after a bit. It'll be dark in the next hour. There's a job to be done outside before that."

She got up, with little care for stiffness and pain, feeling that the price of life might have been much greater, and yet nothing to grudge. He took a good fur from the wall, and threw it over her shoulders, and then, on somewhat unsteady feet, she followed her new lord (if such he were to be) out to where a sky, which she might never have seen again, was rose-coloured with sunset light.

They came together to where the woman lay, face down on blood-soaked grass, her hands still under her belly.

The man looked at the grass. He said: "She must have run round for a bit." Gleda felt no surprise at that. She knew that the swine did so, which it was the custom of her land to slaughter in the same way. She could not be expected to feel dissatisfied by the event. She saw that she had come into the hands of a man of good judgment. One who could take a hint and act promptly.

He picked up the dead woman's fur, which had fallen from her shoulders as she had stumbled about, looked at its condition critically, and hung it over the fence. Then he stooped down, caught her by an ankle, and twitched her over. He said: "You had a good thought...she is heavier than you, but she will take longer to boil. I will have no mess in the house. We must hang her here. You will bring the largest platters that you can find."

Gleda made no reply, but she went back to the house alone. She had never previously (in either life) been involved in the killing of anything larger than a wasp, but the closeness of her own escape modified her reactions now. He seemed to have no fear that she would attempt flight. Well, it would not be possible to recross the river, and to be caught would mean to be back where she was before. She would be a fool to try that.

She went into the kitchen, where she found some large flat dishes which she carried out. While she had been away, he had hung the carcass against a wall. In the new personality which she had assumed, she had certainly had no previous experience in the disembowelling of women; neither had it been a customary occupation in the civilization from which she came. If she did not find it unendurably repulsive now, it must not be overlooked that she was dealing with one who would have considered squeamishness incomprehensible. The hatred that she had felt as the woman had prodded her and licked anticipatory lips had not left her mind, and the thought that the positions would certainly have been reversed but for the man's sound judgment in preferring herself dominated the revulsion which she might otherwise have experienced when the still-warm carcass was slit open and its contents distributed upon the dishes which she had brought.

When he said, as the light failed: "We'd better finish inside. Go ahead, and get a pot on the fire," she went willingly, noticing with satisfaction that he assumed her cooperation, and that she would find the kitchen utensils she might require.

It was some minutes before he followed, and then it was with a half-carcass under each arm, for he had considered that, had he hung it inside, there would have been insufficient space to wield the axe in the low-roofed kitchen. But there was an in-built shelf or table at one end, of its entire breadth, on which he laid his burdens, and proceeded to quarter them, as had doubtless happened to numerous swine before.

Gleda considered him speculatively as he did this. She sought to penetrate his character, which it had become very important for her to know. She reflected that a number of murderers of her previous existence must have treated their wives in the same way. There was Crippen—but she supposed that he had been urged by hatred in what he did. Probably he had had anticipatory pleasure in imagining what he might do, when he had been treated with indifference or contempt. Possibly the memory of indignities inflicted ultimately upon organs which had not been sufficiently complaisant to him had been consolation, even when he passed to the hangman's hands. But this man must have acted on sudden impulse in what he did, on the suggestion which she had made, and now he showed no satisfaction, nor did he appear revolted by his occupation. Beyond a remark upon the size of her kidneys, which he was evidently comparing with those which he more frequently saw, he said nothing, and showed no emotion at all.

This absence of tension was restful to her own nerves, which had been overexcited in the last hours. She did not entirely avoid speculating upon the possibility that she might be on the same table at a near date, but she had no acute or immediate fear.

For the moment, there was food enough. And she felt sure that the cannibalism which she was to share was not customary. The fact that he had taken so extreme a risk for her capture showed how desperate the need for food must have become; it also showed that his people were not adopting the easier expedient of slaughtering the weak or friendless among themselves.

16

It was true that, having obtained what he sought, he had substituted his own wife in what might be considered a most casual, and was certainly an unemotional, manner, but she could not doubt that it had been a sensible thing to do. She could never, surely, criticize him for that!

She thought also the event showed that the wizard who was primarily responsible for her presence there had not made the mistake that she had been inclined to lay at his door. But, all the same, she must not forget a warning which he had given her at an earlier time—that her safety in the new life into which she would be launched must depend on her own wits. He could have no continuing control over what might occur. She became conscious that the man was gazing at her with the knife still in his hand, and a look in his eyes which she did not like. But then he said, as though she had spoken: "Yes, I see it's boiling. Take it off. We'll have fry tonight. But it won't be wasted. We both need a good wash."

CHAPTER III.

Lemno Settles a Debt

GLEDA shared a meal during which little was said. She was cautious, lest she might say the wrong thing, which it would have been easy to do; and he did not appear to observe the silence, nor were his eyes directly upon herself. Had they been married partners for twenty years, he might have acted naturally in the same way.

When they finished, he rose, saying: "I will pay a debt before I am asked. Relf shall hear of this first. He might think—you can clear while I am gone. But no. You shall come with me. It will make it all plain."

He went to the kitchen door (it was there that they had had the meal) and opened it to the cold air. She saw that it was now quite dark outside, though there were stars. She wondered whether those stars would show any difference from their order in her own time. But, if they did, she would be unlikely to see it. Her knowledge of the constellations was too vague for that.

The long fur garment hung loosely from his shoulders. Now, feeling the cold air, he drew it closely together, tying it down the front. Seeing this, she fastened her own in the same manner.

He said: "It's a short way to go. Can you carry a ham?"

"I can carry hers."

He did not appear to observe the tone. But she had learned already that his thoughts were not easy to read. Her predecessor (if she were really destined to take the vacated place) had certainly not been more successful in this. That belly-thrust must have been quite a surprise! It was a pleasant thought, which would have been more pleasant still could she have been quite sure that she would not be surprised in the same way.

They went by a narrow, tree-shadowed path, he going ahead, and she following closely behind. In a few minutes they came to a clearing with a low-roofed house in its midst, similar to that which they had left. There was no fence or garden round it, as she was vaguely aware, her eyes having become used to the darkness beneath the trees. They went up to a door which opened at once, showing a fire-lit interior similar to that from which they had come.

A man faced them, with his back to the light, so that his features were not easy to see, but in build and height he was so nearly alike to the one who stood beside her that Gleda wondered whether there were a single pattern for all the men of that land.

When he saw who was there, he stood aside, saying, in the same toneless manner of speech: "Come in, Lemno, come in."

Lemno took Gleda's burden from her. He handed it to the man, saying: "I have brought you the ham I owe."

"That is good to hear. How did you get it?"

"It is Destra's."

"Destra is dead?"

"Well, I owed you a debt. And I may have got a new wife."

This remark turned their host's eyes upon Gleda. He grunted, then returned to the more urgent consideration. "Is it cooked?"

"No. She was only dead in the last hour."

"Then it soon will be. We have had no more than ten nuts today. We scrape in the forest mud for that which we seldom find. Plera," he raised his voice, "here is food. We must stoke the pot."

Plera came from an inner room. She was a more lithe, better-featured woman than Destra had been. She asked "What is it?" There was eagerness in her voice.

"It is the ham that was owed to us. Destra's ham."

There was a note of incredulous merriment in the reply: "Destra's ham? Her own leg? Then she is dead! It is too good to be true."

There were no more words while, for the next few minutes, man and woman were busy about the hearth. Then Plera looked at Gleda for the first time. She said bluntly: "What are you? You must have been tied by the legs."

Lemno said: "I fetched her from the other side of the river."

There were two cries of surprise. Relf asked: "How could you do that?"

"Well, I did. Hunger drives hard."

Plera looked at her with more appreciative eyes than before. "So there will be more meat to come?"

Lemno shrugged. Gleda was not sure that she liked that. Yet it might have been worse. And it might mean no more than that he would keep his own counsel from those whose whom it did not concern. He said: "I must get back. I have been away from my work all day. When I think of the books that are still unread!"

"Yes, I have been busy. What are you reading now?"

"I am no further than the middle of the twentieth century of what was known as the Christian era during its own time. Others who built on its ruins gave it a worse name. It was a time foul beyond any words which are easy to find. Much of its records are unfit for the reading of decent eyes. Even though we starve, we may be of grateful heart that we live in a better day."

There was animation in their voices which Gleda had not heard before. She saw that they spoke of matters of greater interest to themselves than even a fat ham.

Well, she could tell him more about them than he would be likely to guess. He would be surprised if he knew how much!

But she had been puzzled by his remark that it had been so much fouler than his own time. It seemed a queer boast to make while his friends were putting his wife's ham into the pot—a wife who had been murdered by him. And it must be such an ordinary thing that the question of penalty or concealment did not arise! It must be no more than daily routine, And yet the dual memories which she had did not support the idea without most important qualification. She knew that cannibalism was not the custom of her side of the river, and had not thought it to be on this. Of course, there was the famine, of which she had not heard till she had been brought here. It might go far to justify her capture. But his own wife! She saw that it was no argument to observe that it had been fortunate for her. She must think it out. Or perhaps ask. But she spoke with caution on any matter. Her captor might have many virtues—she hoped he had. But, so far, he had not seemed to be of a chatty kind.

As she thought this, they were returning through the trees, and could already see the light of their own—home? She wondered what sort of home it would be for her.

CHAPTER IV.

A QUESTION IN THE NIGHT

WHEN they had regained the inner room, Lemno turned and looked at her in a speculative way, and there were some silent moments before he asked: "You would be my wife?"

"Have I a choice?"

"You would prefer me to the pot?"

"Yes, I would." As she said it, a fear came. Suppose he should think her to be too cold, too reluctant in her replies? Might he not reject her for that? Suppose he should say at last: "But I am now of another mind. It is to the pot you shall go." Yet to profess desire for him, after the circumstances which had brought her there, might be going too far. She might be unable to give it a genuine sound. She said: "It is more than that. I am alone in a strange place. Who have I to look to but you? I might be of more use than you can yet see."

"A strange place?" he repeated. "I should say the difference is much less than that." She saw that he followed her words with a mind that was keen and alert, and that there had been something puzzling, less perhaps in the word than the tone in which it had been said. The partial consciousness of her earlier existence which had been allowed to remain had a treacherous side, which had nearly betrayed her now. Yet how dare she explain? She said weakly: "There are differences between the way I lived and what I have seen here."

He conceded, fairly enough: "Well, there are some," with no belief in his voice.

She thought it well to add: "There is the fact that I am here."

He took this better. He said: "Where you will remain." They both knew that a return to her own land would be most difficult to contrive. At the best, it would mean going far up the river, or below the falls, seeking a means by which it could be safely crossed, and her way, even before the main difficulties would be reached, would be through hungry and hostile men, who might think of her as a good meal, but, at the best, would spare nothing for her.

He went on, after a pause: "We will give it thought. For tonight, you can sleep here." He pointed to a corner of the room, where there was a small heap of folded furs. He added: "I must work late, having wasted much time for you. If I move about, it will be to make up the fire, which is kept alight. It will not be to disturb you."

She saw that that might be taken as a considerate remark, as perhaps it was, though it could be meant in another way. It was in an effort to establish a more personal contact that she asked: "Why must you work so late? Is it so urgent that it should not have been left?"

He answered readily enough: "You do not guess what I do. It is my toil to inspect, and largely to read, all the books which have been written upon the history of men, just as Relf studies religions and Rakna philosophy; and then I reduce them to what is reasonable to retain. Before the making of books was checked, men had accumulated more than it was possible for them to know, until they lost the ability to choose between a basic principle and a mere detail. Now we proceed in a wiser way, discarding much, and retaining only what can be coordinated on each subject by the mind of a finite man."

She said doubtfully: "Well, it has a sensible sound."

"It may be," he answered, "that the changes we have been able to make will save us from the wreck which has ended all previous civilizations, of which the records are many."

"Did the civilization of which you spoke tonight come to disaster?" she asked.

"So it must have done, or it would continue now. It was, in fact, succeeded by a time of very primitive barbarism, though of superior moral decency; but I have not yet come to that point. I examine all the records we have, going forward from year to year in an orderly way. It was a state of life which was monstrous beyond easy belief, so that its end, by whatever violence, must have been a blessing to those who survived."

He turned away as he said this, and she became discreetly silent, but she thought, as she lay awake, that she had found a way of establishing a possible intimacy such as Destra might not have tried, or, perhaps, been competent to sustain. Her knowledge of the times which he was now studying would be of the greatest value to her in making discussions of intelligent interest to him, though she would have to be careful; it would be easy to reveal too much, and who could foresee what this strong, strange man might do then?

She thought that it was a coincidence of almost miraculous quality that she should have been captured by one whose studies were so engaged, and he being, if she had understood rightly, the only one who was occupied precisely in that way.

Yet was it coincidence? Might not even this have been of the magician's design?

She tried to remember what her conversation with the magician had been, and was both annoyed and frightened to find that it could not be clearly recalled. Was the memory of the past (about which *some* bargain had been made: she was sure of that) to be no better than the recollection of a dream which a man may be unwilling to lose, but which becomes fainter even while he strives to recall it to waking thoughts?

She must endeavour to retain those memories, if necessary by deliberate recollections, when solitary opportunities might allow. But why should Lemno speak with such contempt of the civilization from which she came? She knew that it had developed some evil features: that its records, both of wickedness and folly, were black enough, especially in the incidence of its wars, but surely it had shown better qualities also? Vaguely, she had always thought of her own time as superior even to the centuries immediately preceding. And for him to talk so, with a steak from his wife's haunch already cut for his morning meal!

From these interesting abstract reflections, her mind returned to the immediate future—a dubious prospect of very limited attractions. The position was not one which she could accept passively as beyond her control. Its issue might depend entirely upon her own conduct and her own wits. She had saved herself already by the opportune suggestion that she would be better used as a wife than a meal, but for which she had little doubt that her joints would be distributed now, as those of Destra already were. For the rest, she saw that everything must depend upon the success with which she could fulfil the duties of the job she had taken on.

There came a time when he rose to build up the fire, and as he went back to his place, he looked at her and their eyes met. She knew then, unmistakably, that his train of thought had been close indeed to hers.

Seeing that she was awake, he asked abruptly, though still in the toneless voice which she felt to be no compliment to her: "You are virgin?"

The question was more complicated than he could reasonably have been expected to understand. For a moment it reduced her to silence. Then she replied fatuously: "Yes, I suppose I am."

He showed no sign of observing any ambiguity in this reply, and went back to his books.

Turning her mind to what we may call the left hand of her dual memories, she was glad to conclude that she had probably made a correct reply.

After that, she began to speculate upon what they would eat when Destra had done her part. She did not like the idea of ten nuts a day. It would be no better if she knew that those around her might be considering improvement of their own diet at her expense—and perhaps arguing the prudence of doing so before the meagre ration reduced her weight. She decided that she must aim to become a most desirable wife before that question should become acute. And, for the moment, the empty frying pan witnessed that she had had a good meal; on which thought she slept.

CHAPTER V.

MARRIAGE

SHE waked to find that daylight had come, and that Lemno sat at his table as though he had not moved during the night. Did he never sleep?

Her mind went back to the thoughts which had preceded her own response. Was she a virgin? As a physical fact, as applied to the body which she now had, she was disposed to think that she had given the right reply. Was it what he had wished to hear? That seemed likely too.

He was studying the history of her own time. She wondered with what parts of her world he was becoming familiar. It had been a crudity of the scientists of her time that they had inclined to presume that conditions had been similar in past ages over the whole earth. There might be evidences of a stone age in Nevada or Natal, but why should there not have been a civilization in Tibet at the same time, perhaps superior to anything which had been known subsequently? Even in her own day, in spite of its abnormal development of communications, to which it had sacrificed its prosperity if not its existence, there had been differences between Paris and Central Africa and the interior of Brazil. There was a talking point there, which could be developed without disclosure of what she must not reveal.

Lemno rose, yawning. He stretched his arms upward, so that they were near to reaching the low ceiling of the room. He came over to where she lay. He said: "You lie late." And then, as one who would be just in rebuke, he added: "But we will say there was cause."

She rose at once. She had supposed it to be an early hour. And she had wondered what would be expected of her when she was on her feet what her duties would be.

He gave her a first direction without delay: "You shall heat water first. You shall rub me down."

As the water warmed, he threw off his fur, and strode into the kitchen, a figure of vigorous masculine nudity which was not hard for her to admire. He stood erect and silent on a part of the floor which was slightly beneath the main level, of somewhat different and harder material than its polished boards, with a gutter along the edge. She stood hesitant, and he said, with more impatience than he had yet shown: "Well, will you begin?"

She said "I will do what you wish. It is strange to me."

"It is strange that you do not know where a sponge would be—a sponge which is in your sight now."

As he spoke, she knew; and became aware of a danger she had not realized before. She had two sets of memories, and she had thought that she must use care that those of her distant self—of her real self, she would have said—must not be allowed to fade. She had been dwelling on them, and had not realized that *the two sets of memories could not be active at once.*

Instantly, but none too soon, she became the girl he had captured the day before. She knew what to do now.

She took a sponge which was made of absorbent leaves, sewn together in a flat way, such as she had used all her life, and rubbed him down with warm water from head to foot as he stood motionless there, while a towel of somewhat similar material warmed at the fire. While he dried himself, she dealt with her own body in the same way.

His eyes were on her as she did this, in a fashion that she was not sure she liked, nor yet sure that she would not have. But he did not speak, and the short silence had seemed long by the time she put the towel down, and was conscious of the nervousness in her voice as she asked: "Shall I get breakfast now? Are there no nuts at all?"

"That can wait," he said. He caught her in a strong grasp. "Do you not know what a wife does—or is done to? Well, you are near to learn."

And in the next moments she did.

CHAPTER VI.

THE EVILS OF AN OLD TIME

THEY sat at the evening meal, about which they had agreed that Destra's liver was good.

Gleda ate with relish, the repulsion she might otherwise have felt at the consumption of human entrails being controlled by her hatred of the woman who had felt her own buttock with such greedy anticipation, prodding her like a pig. And the position might have been so precisely reversed! *Her* liver might have been on the dish, and Destra eating it now. It was impossible not to feel some satisfaction at that. And Destra's liver *was* good.

It had been a wonderful day. After the morning consummation, they had talked freely together, and found affinities of mind which (it was easy to guess) Destra had not possessed.

Indeed, a remark he had made during the day—that it was a good thing he hadn't put his knife into the wrong belly—was proof enough that he was contented with her, not only in herself, but in comparison with what might have been.

Now she was asking: "If it's true you've not been cannibals till now, any more than we are on the other side of the river, how did you owe Relf a ham?"

"Relf had a man at his house who fell off a tree gathering nuts."

"*Not really?*" Everyone was so at home in the trees! And the trees were the safest of all.

He did not resent her exclamation of incredulity. He explained: "The only nuts left hanging were on the extreme outer boughs, such as we had never had occasion to gather before."

"Yes…I see. Was he killed?"

"No. But it was unlikely that he would have lived. He was badly hurt. And we were starving men."

"Will you tell me why the times about which you are reading were so bad? Were they worse than these?"

27

"There could be no reasonable comparison. These are probably the best that have ever been. Those were indescribably bad."

"Did they eat each other?"

"I have come on no evidence that they did, so I cannot say. But it is a point of little importance. It is not what they did to the dead, but to the living."

"Do you mean that they had horrible wars?"

"They did. Very horrible ones. But I did not mean that. The worst wars have a heroic side. It was not what they did to their enemies but to their friends by which their values were shown. Can you believe that they used to kill children so that they could move about quickly?"

"But not intentionally."

"You said that as though you know something about them yourself."

"But how could I?"

"No. But, in an unimportant way, what you said was right. They knew that large numbers of children would be killed every week by what they did, though not which children, nor which of themselves the killers would be. And, so far as I have been able to find the facts, they had no reason for speed. They were not frightened of anything. They were not running away."

"As you put it, it certainly has a strange sound. I suppose they would have made it appear in another way."

"No doubt they would. But I have told you the fact, on which their records are clear. They used to count the dead every month, and compare them with what they had done during the same month of the previous year. It must have been a kind of game. But there were other features of that time which were more fantastic, though not worse. There were their laws."

"Did they have many bad ones?"

"It was a question concerning which no man, even though he should give a whole life to their study, could be fully informed. There were too many for that. There was one country, England, where the making of restrictive laws was so excessive that its parliament could not produce new ones quickly enough to suit them, so they delegated authority to many officials who could make laws which their fellowmen must obey, as rapidly as they could dictate or sign them."

"It does sound absurd."

"I have not yet come to the point at which the final result of such a form of civil organization will appear, but some of its consequences in the decade with which I am dealing had been slightly mitigated by the fact that men had largely lost respect for laws which were broken continually, both through ignorance and resentment; and it followed from this that standards of both public and private honour were declining.

"It is particularly curious that while offences against these arbitrary edicts—which, had they not been declared illegal, would not have been wrong at all—were punished with increasing severity, sometimes with fines of fantastic amounts; crimes against individuals, whether of violence or greed, were condoned, and, unless they were persistently committed by the same individual, were hardly punished at all.

"In that country, a period of decadence was also threatened by the fact that the products of a man's labour had ceased to be under his own control, a very large proportion of every income being seized by the state, and spent—more or less—for him, as the governing officials might consider his welfare required, after it had inevitably been much reduced in amount by deductions for their own support, and that of the civil armies which they maintained for distribution, regulation, and control."

"But you don't know how it all ended?"

"Not yet. I expect I shall within a year, or perhaps two. That depends upon how soon the end came."

He went on to explain his work, as that of one of those who had undertaken the coordination of human knowledge, his subject being political history. For that purpose, all relevant books, having been already assembled, were submitted in chronological batches for his inspection. Some of these he would entirely preserve. Some he would summarize. From others he would abstract passages of separate value. But always he would retain a clear purpose of reducing the records of the past to a compass which would be within the possible study and comprehension of one man's brain, within the duration of human life.

Large deliveries of these books were made every four months, when there would be removal of those with which he had dealt. One was now due in two days' time, and—which had never occurred before—he would not be completely ready for the exchange. He had been working against time, having been weakened by shortage of food, and delayed by searching for it, before he adopted the desperate expedient which had resulted in her capture, and it had now become necessary for him to send a telepathic message to postpone the delivery.

She asked: "Can you do that?"

He looked surprised. "Have you no knowledge of telepathy on your side of the river?"

The question caused her a momentary confusion. She had been talking to him in the personality of Marguerite Cranleigh, her mind cautiously alert to avoid disclosure of how much she knew of, and how directly she was interested in, the period of which he spoke. And now she had another experience of how hard it was to transfer to another personality with the memories belonging to it.

But the awkward silence ended when she replied: "We know what telepathy is, but do not practice it in such ways."

"By preference or inability?"

"I don't think we could."

"We have always considered that you were savages; but I should not have thought you to be so primitive as that must imply."

"We are not savage at all. We have a gracious and kindly civilization, sufficient for our own contentment."

"Then you must be easily pleased. Yet you are an intelligent specimen. I will admit that."

It was a compliment which, in view of the final experience of his previous wife, she was pleased to have, though she had already reached a comfortable conclusion that she was in no immediate danger of a similar fate. She saw also (but must not say) that it might be praise, not of those who were in his thoughts, but of the older civilization which he had condemned in vigorous words.

She revealed another unspoken thought when she replied: "Perhaps if she'd had more brains, she wouldn't have had such a good liver."

"It is an interesting speculation. Am I to understand that yours would not be worth frying?"

She felt that the subject might be advantageously changed, and replied lightly: "Yes. Too tough to bite, more likely than not." (She remembered a friend of her far-off days saying how much she disliked a man looking at her as though she were naked. But how much worse it was to be looked at with eyes that seemed to go a lot deeper than that!) She went on rapidly: "Can you really use telepathy to communicate with anyone as you wish, or does it work along special lines?"

"It depends upon vacant receptivity; or stimulation of any mind not too explicitly concentrated."

"I see.... So you don't expect any difficulty?"

"It is most improbable. There would be difficulty if a general referendum were being made."

"Will you do it now?"

"No. Later. When I shall be better able to estimate what further time I still require. But it must be in time to allow of—" He broke off abruptly. He said, with curt emphasis: "Be silent until I speak." And then his eyes changed their focus, as though they looked at a distant thing.

CHAPTER VII.

A NATION ASSERTS ITS WILL

NOW they sat very still, while she thought: "If it takes all this time to say that by telepathy, I call it a slow game."

But, after that, she found that foreign thoughts were invading her own mind, which was soon protesting against them, though with consciousness of the futility of opposition to the force of a hundred thousand contending wills that gained each moment in volume and intensity. Then gradually they came to a unity of resolve as to what they would undertake, to overcome the famine conditions which threatened universal starvation before another season's crop of nuts and fruits should be ripe—and which, even then, would be a meagre subsistence unless the epidemic which had already almost destroyed their swine should be arrested while there were still sufficient remaining alive to breed supplies for the coming year.

The resolve which had now been brought to an apparent unanimity was that food should be sought by penetrating, with whatever violence might be necessary, to the resources of other lands. And, that being agreed, there was next a momentous question to be resolved—in what directions, one or more, should they set out?

For those in Lemno's part of the land, there was the choice of going down the river, below the falls; of going far west, leaving the river at their backs; or of going up the river, and crossing, if they could, above the rapids, to ravage Gleda's people.

Gleda realized that the first of these propositions was not seriously regarded. It was only slightly considered, so that its rejection might be clearly agreed upon. Below the falls there were great stretches of malarial swamps.

To turn their backs on the river was a very different enterprise, for there, beyond the wide, well-wooded plain on which they dwelt, the land rose, not in sudden hills, but by gradual arid, treeless, and windswept slopes, where there was as little to sustain life as there was life to be sustained. But, beyond that, there were great nations in fertile lands, and there was a difference of opinion as to whether they should proceed by threats of violence or peaceful appeal.

To go up the river was obviously the best course.

Above the rapids, two rivers joined. To continue along the nearer bank would be to go far north through their own land, till they would come at last to the impregnable barrier of the great mountain range in which both rivers rose. There would be no profit in that.

But to cross the two rivers, which were separately less formidable, and gentler in their currents, above the rapids, would mean that they must traverse the intervening peninsula, and come at last to Gleda's own country, where no swine plague had raged, though the arboreal harvests had failed, and where the people themselves might furnish a cannibal banquet for starving men.

But—to cross even the tip of the peninsula between? Gleda knew the doubtful peril of that, and wondered, till her mind was borne down by surrounding wills, that, in whatever extremity, it should be considered at all.

The great mountain range was more than a hundred miles away. The two rivers rose about forty miles apart. The space between was a wooded triangle of about two thousand square miles, which, for almost a generation, had not been invaded by human feet.

In the reason for this lay the explanation of much in the constitution of the life around her which had been puzzling to Marguerite Cranleigh, however commonplace, by familiarity, it might have become to Gleda's mind.

There had been, at a quite recent period, a complex civilization, in which the pursuits of science had been honoured and physical laws (as in the far-distant period which Lemno was now studying) had been exhaustively examined, with a view to their alteration and improvement for the benefit of mankind.

There had been a minority who had been unfriendly to these pursuits, to which they attributed the collapse of previous civilizations, but they had been generally ridiculed. They had been called reactionaries, which was regarded as an obviously conclusive word.

At this time there had been a research worker named Ragli, who, having reason to believe that he had discovered a process which would overcome the natural law restricting the size of insects, could not resist the temptation to prove his theory by experiment, from which he expected to gain the respectful publicity which scientists, being human, do not despise.

That which he sought he gained, to a measure beyond his wildest hopes.

He injected his preparation into a mature aphis of a bisexual species, but without producing the effect at which he had aimed. Being unwilling to accept the verdict of a single defeat, he experimented upon others, with equally negative results. But his disappointment was soon over, for these aphides laid eggs. In fact, they laid from 500 to 600 each, and as these eggs produced others, which grew to the size of an ox in less than two days, and as an aphis can eat its own weight at a single meal, it will be seen that it was not a matter which could pass without observation.

Fortunately, the aphis is not formidable (except for its appetite), even when it is of the size of a large cow. There was a short period of liveliness, and then the stench of a great fire, into which many bodies were cast; and after that there was no remaining sign of what had occurred, except in the desolation of many miles of previously cultivated ground.

The author of this mischief expressed no repentance. He said that the massacre should not have occurred. He argued that they would have proved to be useful cows in other respects than size. Were there not species of aphides which were milked by ants? And should men be less shrewd than they?

But this dispute was interrupted by an unexpected and disconcerting event. Another insect, of more formidable character, the tiger beetle, developed to a similarly monstrous size, as did a species of spider.

How these things occurred was hotly contested, and it is needless to debate the two theories which divided scientific support; but there could be no disposition to doubt the facts.

The tiger beetle is much larger than any aphis, and, having a better start, it went further ahead.

The incidence of the event was different. The tiger beetle does not lay 600 eggs at express speed, and those it does produce have a different process of development. These facts would have allowed more time for dealing with what was to prove a menace to the existence of men, had the danger been recognised at an early stage.

As it was, the warfare that followed was of so desperate a character, and, for a time, so dubious of result, that the spiders, which otherwise would have aroused widespread loathing and fear, received literally no attention at all, except from those who felt the grip of their fatal claws.

The beetles had ravaged half a continent before the last one had been turned on to its back, to kick impotent legs above the boughs of surrounding trees. But when this menace had met its end, people became aware that there was a part of the world where no man could rest in his own house without the fear that a green shadow might fall upon it. Then a door or window would be torn away to make entrance space for a huge, hairy, many-jointed arm to enter and grope about for such soft and succulent things as the sensitive hairs upon it would decide fit for the meal of a creature which fed too delicately to swallow more than the squeezed juice of its living prey. It was a menu on which men came to take a high place, and it was the spider's unpleasant habit to scrape out a house very thoroughly before going on to the next.

The war that followed was not, by this time, easy to win, but it was helped by the fact that spiders do not breed very quickly, and that many species (including that of which an enlarged edition had now appeared) have a frugal custom of eating their own offspring, to which they may consider that they have the first right.

But, as their young do not approve of this prompt and equitable termination of separate life, some have a habit of climbing on to their mothers' backs, where they will not be molested, until they have become sufficiently developed for rapid flight and independent life; at which stage some of them will escape, though, if the devil does not take the hindmost, their mother will.

But this program required the presence of herbage high enough to screen their flight, or roots under which they could creep, and, in their enlarged form, cover was less easy to reach, so that the elder generation fattened more than the younger increased.

To hasten the results of this natural process, attacks upon these active and vicious monsters were directed almost exclusively upon the females, by which means it was calculated that the labour of their extermination would be shortened, though scarcely halved, for the females were far the more formidable antagonists.

There came a time when only male spiders remained (or so, at least, it was confidently supposed), and the great majority of these were in the triangular area, bounded by the two converging rivers and the great mountains from which they sprang. By this time, the toll of life had been so heavy, and the destruction of property so great (for it had become habitual for the spiders to tear apart the houses which they searched for victims, after they had been partly frustrated by barricading devices in the lower rooms), that a proposal to terminate the struggle by evacuating the peninsula until, by process of time, the remaining male spiders should die, was favourably received. This procedure had been followed, in the belief that the last female had been destroyed, and that a comparatively short period would be sufficient to clear the land, there being no reason to suppose that increase of bulk would affect the natural process of age and death.

So the great peninsula had been entirely abandoned, and its spiders had been left to find what food they could in the absence of human prey, and to live to whatever age it might have become natural for them to do; and those that remained in the still-inhabited lands, not being numerous, had been exterminated while many houses still stood and many people remained alive.

Two years later, a number of volunteers had crossed the river in canoes, landing on a bare spit of low land that lay at the junction of the two rivers, and cautiously penetrated for some distance into the interior forest to ascertain whether the spiders still lived.

It was a great hazard for a great stake, for if they were dead there was a wide area, largely of fertile forest land, to be reoccupied by mankind But they did not go far enough to see an adult spider. They saw something worse. They saw two young ones, which could not have left their mother's back more than a few days, but which were already of a size to cause a very hurried retreat. It was evident that at least one female had been left alive, and that the pests were breeding anew.

Since then, the great triangle of infested land had been left alone, with the precaution of keeping a lookout higher up the stream, where it rose in the distant mountains, and so far down as it might be possible for a spider to cross, but none had been seen (for this was in a region of ice and snow), and none had appeared in any part of the inhabited lands.

To face them again in the region which they had been left to possess might be a dreadful hazard, but there was the encouragement of alternative possibilities: they might find that the spiders had died out, and that they had come into a land of plenty; or, even though that might be called a poor hope, they might have the good fortune to cross the extreme point of the land without molestation, and find their plunder beyond.

CHAPTER VIII.

A PLAN AGREED

AS confusions of conflicting thoughts gradually cleared and unified, it became evident that, while the main effort would be directed westward, there were some, particularly in the territories adjoining the river, who would prefer the hazards of the eastern venture

Among those who preferred to explore this outlet, a plan gradually took agreed shape by which they would attempt to cross the nearer river, opposite to the end of the peninsula, and either explore its possibilities, or, if the spider peril should seem too great to challenge, cross the second river, and attempt to find food, of whatever kind, in Gleda's native land.

For this purpose, all available fishing canoes (of which there were many in the upper river, before the two joined) were to be assembled facing the peninsula, where they could make any number of journeys necessary before being dragged across it, and launched on the second river, if it should be decided to go farther.

These canoes were not large. They were laborious to make and only useful for fishing, as landings on the spiders' bank had ceased during recent years. The whole of them could not convey more than a few score at one time, so that numerous crossings would become necessary should those willing to join the enterprise be adequate for its success.

The chaos of contending telepathies had quietened and unified as the minds of the great majority of the nation, who accepted the western project, withdrew from Gleda's consciousness, and those more nearly around her separated into their own definite and coherent purpose. Now she became aware that Lemno's mind, apart from the impact of its contiguity, had become a directing force to which others were consenting, and that it had proposed that those who wished to join the enterprise should assemble on the river bank by the evening of the next day. Then she realized, with keener interest, that he was asserting that he had already captured one of the people of the opposite bank; and that this might have contingent advantages, should they find the spiders still in possession of the peninsula, and adopt the alternative plan.

When this had received a vague but general approval, he went on to give the idea that he had secured her loyal cooperation by making her his wife in place of Destra, with whom he had dealt in what he represented without concealment as having been an appropriate manner.

This information having produced a confused, indeterminate reaction, through which hostile criticism if not condemnation seemed to be gaining force, he went on to propose that the material result of his homicide should be at the disposal of those who would join the expedition. The transaction had to be considered not merely as the slaughter of an unsatisfactory wife, which he would be reluctant to advocate as a general practice, but as having both provided him with a better substitute, and the community with food which was desperately needed to strengthen them for the expedition.

Looked at in that comprehensive manner, it was clear again. The population was the same as before, and they had some meat, if not much, at extreme need. There was no necessity to suggest the further possibility that Gleda might be of the same use, for the scale was already down.

As Lemno's will asserted itself to secure a general adoption of this view of the matter, he went on to picture the hazardous exploit by which she had been taken, until he won not merely the admiration which he had earned, but an illogical feeling that it had been adventured rather for the community than himself—a bold hazard to provide meat before the expedition should start, and to obtain a source of information and guidance, if they should adventure the crossing of the farther river.

As the tension of telepathic conflict relaxed, and it became possible to reflect without feeling the pressure of other minds, Gleda said: "It is easy to understand the furs now."

CHAPTER IX.

PRELUDE TO PERIL

SOOTHED by the greater simplicity of Gleda's mind, she fell easily into deep and restful sleep; yet within, the mind of Marguerite Cranleigh busied itself computing and comparing, matching and measuring and analyzing her strange adventure.

Perhaps she had never consciously turned her thoughts to an examination of mankind as a social entity, a single, multi-celled creature crawling blindly through history. Mankind had, it seemed, always been complacently certain that its present was necessarily superior to its past, and that its future would surely bring it another step heavenward. It *always* called itself "civilization." Could this era be called a civilization, when a man could, with impunity, put a knife into his wife's belly and her kidneys upon the grill?

And yet—was not the great telepathic communion she had witnessed a step forward, a truer democracy than that which she had known in her time? The twentieth-century politician was more concerned with popularity than with leadership, and great, obvious trends, like a falling birth rate or a cessation of essential migration would be ignored, or even condoned, if that should serve his popularity. She recalled the case of a strong man called to lead her nation in a death struggle, who, when the fight was won, was rejected in favour of men who easily pledged themselves to what they could not possibly do.

Then perhaps Lemno's was a higher culture after all, for it had both the reverence for the mass mind and the ability to follow a strong leader. And yet—where was the strength in a civilization which possessed, through books, the riches of past great technologies, and yet would undertake an expedition against a stronger, more numerous, better-fed people, and go through a land of monsters in the process, armed with nothing but their wits and perhaps an axe or a bow?

Then she let speculation cease, and her twentieth-century mind sank into that of the sleeping Gleda, and slept restfully with it.

But speculation returned as she sat with Lemno at the morning meal; and when she questioned him as to the adequacy of the resources of his boasted civilization to deal with this animal—no, not animal—with this insect—but they were not insects—say, with this bestial plague, he was frank in reply: "It is certainly true that there was much available in past ages in mechanical equipment and weapons which it might be advantageous for us to have, but which we could not provide, if at all, without too great a delay. But we abandoned these things deliberately to attain a real civilization, and we must accept the disadvantages which result. The price of their production, in every previous attempt at civilized life, has been individual anxieties and almost universal toil. We have tried for something better than that, which need not have been jeopardized now, had we had sufficient prudence to accumulate a reserve of food. But I suppose that we shall do well enough, if we can return before the cold season comes. We must use the nut bags for our minimum of essential needs. We shall have axes and knives and swine-prodders which may be weapons enough. Men must not over burden themselves, being half-starved as they are. The habits of slave civilizations are too entirely abandoned—and were too recently known—to be readily adopted again, even at a great need."

The nut bags were a kind of knapsack used when men climbed to gather nuts for winter storage. They were of more than sufficient size to contain the few personal necessities which Lemno thought it useful to take. Their main load, besides their primitive weapons, would be the meat of which they would soon be relieved, and concerning which Relf's wife, Plera, was already at the door to offer the help of Relf's household for its transport to the meeting place on the bank of the upper river.

Being thanked for this, she showed no haste to be gone. Plera was one who was always willing to talk, and she had a most natural curiosity concerning the events which had brought Lemno a wife from a strange land, and transformed Destra into a neat heap of succulent joints.

Gleda told her freely what had occurred, for she had a friendly smile, which was easy to trust, and added: "I am not the one to complain, knowing that I should be lying there on the slab, had not Lemno made the choice which he did. But it is strange to me that the men of your land should be allowed to kill their wives, and that there should be no law which they have occasion to fear."

Plera looked puzzled. "How could a law prevent that?"

"It mightn't exactly prevent it, if a man were resolved to do it at any cost, or if he thought he could conceal it successfully," Gleda admitted. "But it could punish him if he were caught, and would be an example for others who might be tempted. That hardly needs arguing."

"I don't say it does. But I believe there used to be such laws in terms which were far worse than ours."

"That's just what I'm doubting." Gleda recognized that it would be best to avoid assertion of incredible knowledge. But had not Lemno told her so much? And who would check on the exact limitations of that? She went on: "There was a time called the Christian era, which Lemno was telling me about yesterday. He said it was worse than this. But no one could have killed anyone under their law without the probability that he would be caught and hanged."

"Doesn't that prove what he said?"

"Does it? You mustn't think I'm complaining about what happened to Destra. I know I'm not the one to do that. But—"

"I should think not, indeed!"

"Well, that's what I said. But—"

"There's no but about it. It needed doing, whether he'd caught you or not."

"Do you mean she was such a bad woman?"

"I don't mean that she did the kind of things that laws used to punish. There must often have been excuses for them. What they called temptations. But she did worse things. She used to make Lemno's life wretched with her tongue, and in other ways. It went on until Relf made some excuse to get her by herself at our house, and when she went home she had less skin on her buttocks than when we put her across a chair. She was a lot better for that, especially after we made her come next week and thank us for what we'd done."

"Doesn't that just show what good things punishments are?"

The question reduced Plera to a short silence, after which she said frankly: "But it wasn't quite the same thing. You see, we *knew* what we were doing. It wasn't like strangers butting in, and talking as though a law were something above themselves, without using their own judgment, like serving a god. And when you talk of killing people you've got nothing against, because they killed someone who may have driven them mad—well, I should say that the first killing might have been bad or good, but the second would be bad beyond doubt at all."

"You seem to take no account of it being a warning to other killers."

41

"Well, as to that, you'd have to prove that there'd be more than twice as many killings if there were no punishments, before you'd have a leg to stand on. And even then there'd be the question of whether it's right to do things that you know are wrong because there may be good results in another way. But that wasn't really the argument that made us decide that no civilization could be any good unless it were without laws. It was the fact that people felt that they'd got to act according to law, even though they might think it bad for the case they tried. They thought law was superhuman; and subhuman was what it was."

"I think you have overlooked one thing in what you were saying—that murderers were not usually violent killers of provocative pests. They often had much meaner motives, and their crimes were very cunningly done."

"Then it must have been very hard to be quite sure they'd got hold of the right man. And very tempting to make a guess, after all the fuss and trouble there'd been; and those who guess may guess wrong.

"Don't you think that if it had been left for general discussion— if anyone wanted that—or for those who knew most about it to deal with it in their own way, or to leave it alone, there might have been better justice, as well as a lot less misery?"

"It does sound reasonable," Gleda conceded readily. "It seems to me that it would depend most upon the characters of those in whose hands it would be left." Perhaps, she thought, laws are good for those who would not otherwise conform to civilized ways, but no civilization can be secure until it has arrived at a higher stage. But it also occurred to her, none too soon, that she might easily reduce her own popularity by too warm a defense of an ancient time, which should be nothing to her. And, beyond that, she was less than sure that these people were wholly wrong.

CHAPTER X.

A Question About Children

"PLERA spoke as though she were coming with us," Gleda said, as she and Lemno were packing their bags. "I shouldn't have thought the women would be so keen on it, seeing how dangerous it's likely to be. Will there be anyone else from there?"

"I doubt it. There's only Relf's father, who's getting feeble, and his sister, who's rather lame. But as to the women going, you must remember how hungry they are. I don't say they'll all want to go over the river. But there won't be many round here who won't get as far as the bank. And I expect they're hoping for a bit of our meat, which most of them can't possibly get."

"How about leaving the children?" As she asked this natural question, it occurred to her for the first time that she had seen none; but, after all, in two homes only— And yet, Destra's insides had shown signs of—

"The question, he said, "doesn't arise, except at the rearing-pens, where proper arrangements will doubtless be made. But they are too far away for anyone to join our expedition from that district."

"You don't keep your children at home?"

"No. Do you keep yours? But we've no law about that now, and every year there are more people who rear them themselves, although it makes their lives harder in many ways."

"You weren't allowed to before?"

"Not when we were under the curse of law. It wasn't likely that a bureaucracy, when it became well established, would leave people to make their own choice in such a vital matter as that. The law was that every young married woman must contribute three children— one every four years—and if she should fail to do that, she would be removed, and the man provided with a more amenable wife."

"That was hard on her, if she couldn't."

"It was expensive, but not as bad as it sounds. People have been adroit in all ages to avoid the worst effects of the laws they are weak enough to let other men lay on their backs. There were many women who liked to produce children—or who made a trade of it—and they would sell them at the best price they could get. It meant that occasional surplus children had to be destroyed, which everyone regretted, but they argued that it was the law, and that respect for law is the foundation of every civilized state. So it may be; and that was why we blew the foundation up."

"Have you got any children there?"

"Destra had two. She would not keep them here, so they had to go. Their numbers are branded beside the door. In that respect, the old system has been continued, it not being worth anyone's while to object."

"But, if I have a child, I can keep it here?"

"Yes. It's a free country now."

"I don't wonder people came to hate laws."

"Yes. I suppose what they used to call communism in the era I was talking about yesterday will always defeat itself in the end in that way. But it's a hard road. I've got to go out now, and arrange for some of our neighbours to take the canoe. We shall be loaded enough, without that."

CHAPTER XI.

Mainly Concerning Spiders

WHATEVER differences there may have been between Gleda and Marguerite, they were alike in knowing very little about spiders, and, had they been asked, they might have agreed in saying that there was very little to know.

They might have described them as small black creatures (probably as insects) having an excessive number of legs, and a habit of spinning webs in which they caught flies and other small creatures on which they fed. Marguerite would have added that she had been told that female spiders sometimes eat their husbands when they have finished with them for other purposes.

Either of them would have been surprised to learn that they are not insects, but an entirely separate order of creation, and that a list of twenty thousand would not exhaust their known varieties, with differences far greater than those which divide mammals, or birds, or fishes; so that there is more unlikeness between one spider and another than between a cat and an elephant, in size, in structure, in colour, in diet, and in the conditions in which they live.

There are spiders with only two lungs; there are some with four. Their eyes vary in number and in position. They may have essential organs relegated to the lower end of a limb.

They have possessed the whole earth, from Arctic to Antarctic regions. Some species live in the highest mountains, some beneath rivers, some in the sea. Some catch their food in webs, some lie in wait to leap upon it, some chase it and run it down.

In intelligence, comparisons between them and the human race are not easy to make. In adaptability to environment, they have shown superiority. In numbers, they have so great an advantage that it would be an incalculable underestimate to say that they are a hundred millions to one. To a detached observer of our small planet, it might seem evident that men, in comparison, are of no importance at all.

The points on which all their species agree are those which separate them furthest from humankind. They have no heads; their lungs, few or many, are in their hindquarters; their organs of generation are not confused with those of evacuation, but in separate parts of their bodies. Compared with the body of a spider, that of a man may be considered a clumsy experiment, the mistakes of which were not repeated when the next creation was put in hand. Incidentally, they disprove the idea of evolution as a blind force, for there are respects in which nothing but intelligent, fore-thinking design could have brought them to what they are.

Could man and spider bridge the immense physical and ethical distances that divide them, so that they could debate their relative positions in creation's scales, the spider might assert with confidence that his bodily structure is superior, and that he has shown at least equal intelligence in the methods by which he has possessed the earth; while ethically man could only hope to avoid an argument that he could never win, for though there may be occasions when the hunger of a female spider will overcome her kindlier impulses, so that she will eat a husband whose use is done, and though there may be some of her race who eat a proportion of young they tend, they practice no cruelties upon one another which can be considered seriously comparable to those which are the continual record of the dealings of man with man.

It is true that the differences among the various forms of sentient life on the earth are so trivial that it might seem futile to any really different being that such an argument should be raised at all. They all pass through a period of growth and immaturity; their organs are similar; they live by feeding; their lives are occupied in providing that food, and producing a new generation in kindred ways; they grow old and die. There are a hundred similarities for every difference which can be found, and these similarities are more fundamental.

But the spiders could argue with some confidence that while they sustain life by slaughtering other species, they do not descend to the crudities and brutalities of the slaughterhouses of mankind, but kill the creatures they require, whether caught by web or chase or a sudden leap, with an injection of poison which is instant in its effects.

They could argue that their method of reproduction—the eggs in the spun cocoon—is immeasurably more civilized than that which retains the foetus in the mother's body, to be expelled at last in an unsightly manner, dangerous and painful both to mother and child.

They might even be indelicate enough to allude to the fact that their organs of copulation are not in the rear of their bodies, which they reserve for inferior purposes, but are centrally situated in the female, and, in the male, at the end of the left arm, so that (should they be silly enough to attempt it) it would be without embarrassment that they would explain the facts of life to the young.

These are points of superiority to which reply would not be easy to make; and it might be added that there is overwhelming advantage in being so much smaller, size only existing relatively, and this difference meaning that they inhabit a planet millions of times larger and more complex than that which must be good enough for mankind.

But this last advantage had been suddenly and completely lost by some members of the Arachnida, which had found themselves in a dwarfed world, in which the giant trees had shrunk, in which movements had been impeded, and in which food had become much harder to secure.

Either Marguerite or Gleda would have said carelessly that spiders are black, though a challenge of that might have brought vague memories of brown or speckled bodies (or were they crane-flies which also have legs which are much too long?), this being one of many matters concerning these creatures on which Gleda had much to learn.

For these enlarged spiders, which, at an earlier time would have been said to be more or less of the family of the *Sparassidae*, and of the species *Micrommata viridissima*, were green, with a darker patch, yellow-edged, on the forward abdomen, over the heart; while the male (as with all spiders) was smaller; and its abdomen was splendid with scarlet and yellow bands.

Accustomed to hold with firm feet to the surface of a wind-swayed leaf, to which their colour would blend invisibly till they should leap upon some incautious insect, how should they have adapted themselves to survive in a world which had ceased so radically to be adapted to them?

CHAPTER XII.

A GOOD CAUSE TO FEAR

IT was late afternoon when Lemno's little party came to what was already a large crowd on the river bank.

They had been met some miles before by a gaunt, hungry gathering, which threatened trouble until Lemno pointed out to them both that the meat was uncooked, and that he would resist with deadly violence any attempt to take it from him. "If any of you make that kind of trouble," he said, "there'll be more meat for the pots tonight, so you'll please us all if you do."

It was a method of relieving famine which they could not be expected to welcome, and they restrained themselves, from that or other considerations, until the river showed through the trees.

Lemno said afterwards that it was the absence of law which had prevented riot, at which Gleda, who had feared violence from that defect, had expressed surprise. But he explained that law had continually proved unequal to restraining an excited mob. But among these folk, there was the general knowledge that good conduct was a personal obligation to the community, with a constant fear that, should they misconduct themselves, they would be subjected to private justice, and might even be doing something which would tend to lead the whole community back to the hated bondage of law. In that paradoxical sense, it might even be said that the fear of law had been their restraint. But it is relevant to observe that good manners were always more general among those who practiced the private duel.

The canoes made their first crossing as darkness fell. Most of them were small, and the total load was not more than seventy men. Lemno and Gleda were among those who were first to cross. As they went down to the bank, they passed a caldron, hanging over a low wood fire, in which Destra's bones were being boiled, to make a thin soup which was doled out to those who were first to venture—

and might be last—for it had been agreed that they should explore the dangers of the peninsula before there would be a general invasion, or a final decision as to whether its interior should be occupied, or if it should be rapidly crossed to exploit the possibilities of the land beyond.

It was a hazardous adventure, and there had been some delay in obtaining the necessary numbers of volunteers. They must enter a land which had been abandoned for many years, and might be occupied by such a multitude of the giant spiders that their weapons would be no more than abortive toys; or they might find that the spiders were dead, in which case the land might have suffered from the same drought as their own—there must be expectation of that—but might still be a reservoir of essential food, abounding with swine which the epidemic had failed to reach.

If the spiders were there, they must attempt to cross the tip of the peninsula without attracting attention, which might be done safely in the night hours; and there were some, for this reason, who would have preferred that nothing should first be tried which might stir attention to what they did. But yet, if the land were empty—no, it was not a doubt they could leave unproved.

Among those who went on this hazardous enterprise, Gleda observed, with correct appreciation of how the distinction arose, that she was the only woman. It had been assumed that other women would not be chosen, and equally so that she should be there.

In the doubt and hazard of what must be done on the next day, it is not surprising that they lay awake, nor that they talked during the night.

Lemno said: "If the spiders have left the land, or are not too many for us to slay, there should be food enough for our needs, so that—"

"You have not thought that other men may have been there sooner than you."

"There could have been none, unless they came from your own land."

"I do not think any will have done that. We are too greatly afraid. Also, there has been no shortage of food."

"Well, we shall soon know when the light comes."

"It is coming now," she said, for while they talked the dawn showed dimly above the trees that lined the farther bank of the river they had not crossed.

The point of the peninsula on which they had landed was bare and rocky, giving clear sight over a triangle of ground which was half a mile wide where the forest rose; but the growth was denser than any which they had been accustomed to see. For here the trees had risen at their own will, and there were many saplings and brambles and bush between the boles of those which had been there when the land was left free from human control.

As the light widened, they rose, somewhat stiffened with cold, in spite of their close-thonged furs, and Lemno moved along the forest edge to direct the advance. Gleda followed closely behind.

They were to go forward in parties of two, which, should they all be able to maintain a straight course, would separate them more widely as the breadth of the peninsula increased. They were to aim at reaching a place at which it narrowed again, owing to an eastward bend of their own river; but, in any event, they were not to go forward after midday, so that they would get back before darkness came.

They were cheered, as the light increased, by the sight of a hard-shelled fruit, much like a pomegranate in appearance, which lay thickly scattered under some of the trees. At least they would not starve during the day.

When they had eaten, and were about to start, Lemno threw off his fur.

"We cannot be cumbered with long garments," he said, "having to break through such tangles of untamed growth, even if we do not have to take to the trees."

Gleda did the same with reluctant hands, shivering in the morning breeze.

"You will not feel it," he said, "when you are moving, and out of the wind that vexes the forest edge. We will start at once."

She noticed that he spoke with more animation than she had been accustomed to hear, except when he talked of his work, or had been sporting with her.

She said: "It is strange that when we are nearest death we are most alive."

He understood her at once. He said: "That is only true when men approach death, rather than when it approaches them.

"It may be a reason why men in earlier days approved dangerous living, or even war with their own kind. But such wars cannot be without evils of other kinds. It is ever the best who die. Look at those who are with us now."

That was easy to see. The volunteers had been those who were most virile of mind and body. Quality rather than numbers was staked on their safe return.

She did not answer, for, by now, they had adjusted the knapsacks to their naked shoulders, so that their hands were free to use the knives which might be needed to cut their way. Lemno also had a long pig-spear, at which she looked dubiously.

"It will be awkward if we have to take to the trees. Is it worth while?"

"Perhaps not against the spiders. Hiding may be our best chance, should we see any of them. But if we could get meat—"

"Yes. If there are pigs which will stand still to be killed."

She spoke with knowledge, for the pigs of both their lands were dealt with in the same way, being no more than half wild. They were first driven into enclosures by long lines of beaters, who bore these spears—pig-pokers they were called—which it was seldom necessary to use, and which were only intended to prod them on.

"It is a small chance," he said, "or else none."

It proved to be impossible to make rapid progress. The woods, which had once consisted only of orderly, cultivated trees, with clear, grassy spaces between, where the swine would graze and root, had become choked with saplings and brambles and coarser weeds.

They had calculated that, as they went forward, fanning out as the land widened, though it might not be easy to advance straightly, they would be assisted by the sight of companions on either side. But the thick growth made it impossible to see for more than a few yards, either to right or left. They must depend upon sound rather than sight, and sound was dangerous till they were assured that the woods were clear of menace to them.

"I will go first," Lemno said, after a time. "It is no advantage to break through in a double way."

This was after Gleda had torn her left arm on so large a thorn that the blood dropped to her feet. She said: "Well, I can help." She went on, sometimes at his side, sometimes behind. They tried to go straight ahead, rather than avoid obstacles, thinking that any other method would soon bend them aside.

At times they stopped where a few nuts with full kernels might be combed out of the grass, but they saw that, whatever might be in front, either spiders or swine, the drought had been as disastrous here as in their own lands. The only difference was that they appeared to be the first to glean what the drought had spared.

As to the swine, Lemno said, after a time, that there was no more than a poor hope: "They would make aisles through this tangled growth."

But, when hope was low, it was to such an aisle that they came. It was not precisely in the direction at which they aimed, but enough so to induce them to take advantage of it. After a time, it widened into indistinctness, where the ground became rocky and poor, and there were few trees, and insufficient undergrowth to obstruct the movements of pigs or men.

Then they came to a forest pool, where they drank gladly, and beyond that the trees were crowded and the undergrowth dense again, and they came to another of the trampled aisles that the animals made, but while they were still a short distance away, Gleda said suddenly: "Look! Look over there—there are three!"

So there were. Three pigs feeding together on a patch of grass that showed fresh and green from the recent rain. And, as she spoke, as in a flash, they were gone.

Lemno said: "That was queer."

She answered vaguely "Yes. They weren't long about it."

"It wasn't only that," he replied. "I don't know how the pigs behave in your land, but in mine they'd have taken the aisle, and trotted along it in no great hurry unless they were followed up. But they dashed into the undergrowth as though a devil were at their tails. And there can be no men hunting them here. And they are the only three we have seen in two hours—and fruit lying on the ground."

Gleda heard this with a frightened heart, for its meaning was easy to see. The pigs were few. Enemies must be keeping their numbers down. They were frightened, and had learned that to take instant cover was the one method by which life might be prolonged. And she and Lemno were walking without concealment, and with no equal capacity for instant disappearance should danger threaten.

Yet she answered bravely enough: "May it not mean only that they have become unused to the sight of men?"

What could they do but go on with more watchful eyes? As to that, the trouble was that they must have eyes for the way they took, and for the boughs they must bend aside. That would be less the case if they should take the aisle which they could not doubt that the pigs had made, but might yet be the way to a quick death. How did they know that its farther end might not be watched by a huge bulk with eight patient, unwinking eyes, and a hairy arm outstretched, perhaps with a claw which would be instant to snatch, and pinch, and pierce, and lift its victim to the quick death of the poison-prong.

Lemno paused in hesitation. Had they learned enough? Should they go back?

"No," he said. "It is too vague as yet. We must go on. But I will lead, breaking the way. You must have eyes only for any danger ahead, trusting me for the steps you take."

He had a cold fear at his heart, but he was conscious of the obligation of honour. Was he not of the aristocracy of his kind?

"Did you see a spider," he asked, "in the old days?"

"No. I was too young to go to the war."

"I was not. But I was one who survived. I was so near to death at one time that I was touched by the spines of a groping arm, which would have taken me had not a comrade come first into its claw, while I could do no more than to hack at it, as it withdrew. The fresh green that the rains have brought will make them harder to see, for that is just the colour they are."

"Is it any use carrying that pig-poker now?"

"Not for the pigs. They are far too wild. But I will keep it for any good it may be.

They went on, but Gleda found that it was easy to shake with fear.

CHAPTER XIII.

A Spider Has a Surprise

WHEN Dullo Ragli had turned his learned attention to aphides, and increased their size, he had not meant them either evil or good. He had not considered very intelligently what the consequences might be for his fellow men, and for the aphides he had cared just nothing at all.

As for the spiders—they had been a side issue. He had certainly meant no good or evil to them. But, had he been asked, he would probably have replied, and believed, that their increase in size, which had been a curse to mankind, had been a potential blessing to them.

Actually, it had been much the reverse, and had they not belonged to the most adaptable family of all the creatures that contend for life on the earth, their careers would soon have been done.

There was now a spider, ten feet high at the upmost curve of her cephalothorax—a half-grown spider, now in her second year—who would have been emphatic in agreement on this, had it been put to her in the right way.

She was too young to have faced the difficulty of setting up a cocoon (which her mother's ingenuity had surmounted, or she would not have been there), but she was conscious of hunger as a companion which seldom left her, although, being a spider, she had not the mammalian's weakness of needing anything up to four meals a day.

Any time during the last eighteen months, she would have been glad of three meals a week, which she did not get.

The pigs had become few, and those which remained would shoot like lizards from bush to bush, and there was nothing else in the land of size and kind to supply a meal for creatures as large as she. She could wait patiently, hour by hour, day by day, at a chosen point, never moving unless to make a lightning dash at some crea-

54

ture which would come near without observing her in her stillness and blending green, and for whom carelessness would be certain and instant death. But too often the day would pass, and no creature would come.

Having no conscious memory of her ancestors' lives, she had no knowledge of the pleasure of holding on to a swaying leaf, green as her invisible self, and waiting—so short a time!—for the victim that would always come: of the swift outward leap, of her palpi seizing the prey in their deadly claws, of the quick lift to the poison-injecting dagger under her two rows of eyes, and then the sucking of the juices of the anaesthetised victim while it still lived, into a mouth which was formed to take nourishment in no other way

She would still take her prey more or less in the same manner, unless she should be forced by extreme hunger to search under the trees, pulling bramble and branch aside. But there would seldom be any profit in that.

Her ancestors had had a much better time while there had been men to hunt. Men who had been easier to catch than the pigs, and who had recognized their inferiority by ignominious flight, where the quadrupeds held their ground and had not been entirely unable to exist beside their monstrous enemies. Not that she would have troubled to distinguish between them; and, indeed, from the spider's standpoint, the difference was too slight to be regarded seriously.

That men and pigs had their lungs in the wrong part of their bodies might not be a cause of contempt; the thorax may do well enough for them, though the abdomen is clearly the better place.

But to have no poison fang with which to prepare your meal in a seemly way!

To have to masticate food!

To have only two eyes!

Only two double-jointed legs!

And how could forelegs or arms be compared to palpi, with their flexibility, their sensitive spines, their final claws! (At least, claws for herself, the male palp ending in another way.)

The structures of men and pigs were too closely alike, as seen by a higher type, for them to be regarded otherwise than as very closely allied, or in any other light than as potential meals. The green body, which had scarcely moved for two days, became rigidly still, for two humans were approaching now.

They saw when it was too late. The palpi came down with their great claws piercing the man's neck so that he lacked even a moment in which to scream. In one continuous motion she raised him to the fang which was between eyes and mouth, and which would give unconsciousness of his coming death, and the hard plates which were round her mouth closed upon him, to squeeze his juices into that eager receptacle.

But, as she did this, she became aware that his companion had not fled, as he should have been certain to do, but was hacking desperately at a joint of one of her hind-most legs.

She felt pain, which she did not like. She felt her leg giving way, which would have been of greater consequence had she not seven others to bear her weight.

She dropped her dying prey, and swung round with agility, controlling her many legs as easily as a man would have managed two. But, as she did so, she became aware of another foe, and a worse wound. There was a man at her rear side who was driving a pig-poker into her abdomen. Grasping it with both hands, he pushed hard. It went deeply into one of her lungs. She had no pleasure in that, nor any thought of the glory of war. She had too much sense to get hurt for lust of battle, or of revenge. In an instant she clambered upward, and out of reach.

Lemno held on to the poker, which came free, drenching him with green liquid, which had an evil stench. He saw the spider clamber up between trees, grasping the boughs on either side with her many legs. She disappeared at once, running fast over the tree tops. The man she had killed had gone too. She had been too cool and quick, even in the astonishment of attack and the pain of wounds, to forget her meal.

Lemno said to Gleda (who had come up almost as soon as he, though too late, with a bare knife) and to the companion of the dead man: "I can see you can be trusted when the need is great. We saw the beast before you did, and were about to creep quietly away (if we could have done that) when you came on the scene, so that we must alter our plans."

"It was bravely done," the man answered. "I supposed I was near to death."

"Well, you did not flinch. But, for myself, there is no need to say much. For I have known these spiders of old, and she would not have fought, having got a meal, unless she were cornered, or lost her temper, as they are not unlikely to do. And this one was not more than half grown, though I will allow that the females are worse than the males. They grow to a larger size, and have claws which the males lack."

The man said that this was not hard to believe, for though the spider had been big enough, it had been smaller than some in the tales he had heard. He added: "You must have come at a slant to have been so near."

"Yes. Or else you. But I think that we should go back now, and that we should keep together now that your companion is dead."

So they agreed to do; and meanwhile the spider, having got well away, had sucked the juice from a crushed victim who might be dead or alive, but was too drugged to know which. So she had her way without protest from him, and dropped the husk through the trees, to be devoured by inferior creatures. Even if she had been starving, she would have had no more use for it.

Her wounds could not be helped. They must heal, as they could, in their own ways.

She met another spider, who had been of her brood, and with whom, as yet, she was friendly enough. She told him what had occurred, in the soundless language which spiders have, leaving nothing out, for it had not the limitation of words.

Her description of the creatures which she had seen for the first time drew attention to their exterior peculiarity. They had loose heads. Even the pigs were not quite like that.

In that particular they were most like the insects that her ancestors had hunted for food. She did not know this, but regarded them in the same way.

She showed also that they were of an extraordinary viciousness, not consenting to be killed in a quiet, natural manner. It was the annoyance with which a butcher might regard a rebellious boar, having been used to the acquiescence of sheep.

Her companion did not wait when he knew the tale. He was too hungry for that. He set off, over the tops of the trees, at a rapid pace, in the direction from which she had come.

The boughs swayed and creaked, and sometimes broke amid the clutching of many legs, which he did not heed at times he must have leaped as much as fifty feet, or perhaps more. But that was easy to do.

CHAPTER XIV.

LIVELINESS IN RETREAT

THE man whose comrade had perished, Biro, was nervously talkative as they went back together (so far as conditions allowed, for they now kept to the denser growths, and progress was hard and slow), which may have come from the ordeal he had survived.

He assumed that there would be no further attempt to penetrate spider-infested woods, and speculated only upon whether it would be possible to get everyone across the peninsula before they would be heavily attacked by inhuman foes.

Gleda answered him with a divided mind, having no desire for a repetition of what she had seen, but being reluctant to encourage invasion of the land where her kind lived.

Lemno, to her surprise, was not only quick to understand her feeling, but to give it more support than she had expected to hear.

He said: "You can have no wish to return to your own land as one of those who would spoil and slay?"

She felt that a wrong reply would be easy to make, but yet answered frankly enough: "Yes. I had hoped that we should have found this place to be fruitful, and that the spiders would have been dead by now."

"That was natural. I had the same hope. You must not suppose it is settled yet."

She felt that she had done well not to make a more evasive reply, and the more so as he went on: "When food is scarce, there must come a time when some will die, or else all. And, I would rather eat men of another race than my own kin—or to make a meal of those who are wounded or slain, as, if there be fighting enough, both sides may be able to do.

"But I would rather eat pigs than men. And I would rather kill spiders than those of a closer kind. Even at a great risk that would be my choice. But I am not sure that it will be a popular one, so you should be prepared (being one of us, as you now are) to assert your will to its full strength."

"So I will," she said, "having your support beyond what I could hope."

He replied: "You will know me as the days pass," at which she felt closer to him than she had been at any moment since he cut the rope from her legs.

As they talked, they pushed their way through the densest undergrowth they could find near enough to the right way, Lemno going first, as before, though with help from her, and Biro keeping near their side.

They would have said that they were alert for any warning of sound or sight, as they had enough reason to be, but exchange of thought must distract the mind, and it was Biro who was first aware of the terror above their heads.

He asked in a tense voice, vibrant with fear: "What's that?"

In the next moment they knew. There was a green monster scrambling with many legs over the tops of the trees, and this was at as bad a moment as could have been, for they were crossing a patch of ground which was stony, with little growth.

Then several things happened quickly.

The spider paused for an instant, judging the leap which he must make to pass over the open space. And then he saw the three breaking into the densest thicket on the farther side.

He could leap with a great speed, judging exactly with his many eyes for the limited range of their multiple vision, and having good control of his numerous and very sensitive many-jointed legs. There was a moment when he would not have jumped, knowing he would be too late. But the next, there was something he had not expected to see, and he leaped with a speed and judgment which would not fail.

The fact was that the bushes into which the three fugitives pushed were not what they would have liked them to be. They were dense enough to make progress slow, even to such efforts as theirs, but so scant that, almost at once, they saw light on the farther side. And they found that the narrow shelter was already occupied.

It was a bad day for those pigs.

How could they doubt that they were being hunted by these humans who had disturbed them before? There was a quick sideward scurry, a dash backward to cross the open space from which their enemies came, and, as the foremost bolted out, the spider leaped down with unerring aim.

In the same instant that the pig became aware of the pressure of squeezing jaws, it met the stare of eight unwinking eyes, felt the sting of the poison fang, and lost consciousness.

Its companions swerved madly back to the shelter of the bushes and came upon Biro at a speed which, in that crowded place, he could not have avoided. He advanced his poker at such a height that its point entered the mouth of the first rushing pig. Its impetus transfixed it, while it bore Biro backward into a discomfort of many thorns for his sun-tanned back.

The poker tore down the grunting throat, from which came the changing note of a high squeal, which ceased next moment, as the sharp point went on, in its slightly downward course, till it came out in the hinder part of the animal's belly.

Biro exerted his utmost strength to pull out the spear, alert for flight from the huge green, scarlet-banded monster which could be glimpsed through the swaying of large-leaved boughs. But Lemno, coming to his side, said quietly: "You needn't worry about the spider now. They're not often troublesome when they're well fed. There's a bit of luck for us here, in more ways than one."

He caught the shaft of the poker, put his foot on the animal's head, and gave Biro the necessary help to finish pulling it out.

As it drew free, the blood came in steady spurts, both from the pig's mouth and the hole where the points had emerged, and its kicks became rapidly feebler.

Biro obviously felt that he had done a good job; but, if Zeus had been looking on, he might have contrasted the brutal crudities of human methods with the exact and instantaneous execution that the spider had dealt, and given the award of a higher standard of civilization to him of the many legs.

Meanwhile Lemno, after his first confident announcement, had a moment of doubt. The spider was already dropping a flaccid body, which it had squeezed flat and sucked dry.

"We needn't tempt him."

They made off at the best pace they could, the legs of the dying pig around Biro's neck, and his knapsack on Gleda's arm.

CHAPTER XV.

AN AGREEMENT TO DISAGREE

THE three who came back with the tale of a comrade lost, and the carcass of a dead pig, found that they were the only ones who had anything to report, either bad or good.

The others returned, some sooner, some not till the darkness fell, without having seen any creature larger than a wood pigeon, or heard anything more formidable than a jay's screech. They had found food of kinds, but they had still a very good appetite for the pork which was roasted and shared round the wood fires which they kindled fearlessly, for the green hunting spider is not inclined to activity in the night. The unfortunate animal had been plump, and there was something, if not much, for all.

As they ate, Lemno advanced the idea that they concentrate upon the reconquest of the peninsula, relying upon their ability to destroy the spiders, and calculating that there would be sufficient pigs to lift the shadow of starvation which had fallen upon them.

This was contrary to the resolution of the previous day, which had been a clear decision that they should go forward across the second river, if the spiders should still be living. Now spiders had been encountered, and one man was dead. But—there was the argument of the good meal.

The pig had done its first good office by assembling the hungry men. Round Lemno's own fire, he had invited Relf, and a few others whom he aimed to influence first, to divide the carcass. Gleda was, of course, there to support him. She thought that he put the idea forward in very plausible words, but could see that it was not warmly received.

Relf was most willing to entertain it, but even he gave it no more than cautious consideration. "You will not overlook," he said, "that the whole land must be cleared, or we shall have done nothing.

The land is vast, and we have two thousand men at the most, and we do not know how many spiders there may be now."

Lemno shrugged. "They may not be numerous. More than fifty square miles must have been penetrated today, and no more than two young ones were seen. They may have found conditions too adverse for any great increase to have occurred. But what's the alternative? To slaughter men, to pick their bones, and to have their land. And they will have different ideas, and our bones may make soup for them."

"Is that all the reason you have?"

"No. I would rather kill spiders than those of my own kind. I would rather eat pigs than men."

"It is not an argument by which our women would be convinced."

"I suppose not. Though some would. You will consider that there are few women among us. It is not a matter for those who stay behind to decide."

Relf agreed that that would give the proposal a better chance than it would otherwise have. For the best of women would think first of what would be safest for their own men, and last of what would be the more likely to fill their own bellies, and very few would allow altruistic arguments to divert their minds, as is the common weakness of men.

In the end, he said: "Well, it may be worth trying. We could give it up and still go over the river, should spiders be too many, or pigs too few. But you may find our men hard to persuade, one being dead in the first bout, and the spiders having no loss at all."

So, with this consent, they got together a few who would give support, choosing those of strong wills, and whose minds were active and clear, and they began to think together, in a way which must soon gain access to other minds.

Gleda was among these, being told by Lemno that she should exert her will to the utmost, which might be useful, if she could sustain it.

They fought together for some time in this way, but though they would not yield, they could not prevail, a large majority preferring the hazard of human foes. But when it was realized that neither side was willing to give way, an idea arose and gained ground, that some might go one way, and some another, as they might prefer; and this was at last agreed upon, the majority giving way to this extent, in a general belief that dissenters would soon be glad to join them when they had experienced the conditions of warfare against the spiders.

While the debate proceeded, the canoes, which had been occupied in fishing during the day, were bringing more people across, at a rate that made it evident that the work would be completed, and transit to the farther bank be in operation, before the dawn.

The night was still dark when Lemno, who was now tacitly accepted as leader in the campaign against the spiders, and who seemed indifferent to rest or sleep, had completed the count of his own forces as 519 men and three women, Gleda having been joined by Plera, and an active young widow named Jalna, who may either have aimed at forgetting the sorrow of a recent bereavement, or of obtaining another spouse by joining herself to this male assemblage.

Being already satisfied that spiders were not numerous at the tip of the peninsula, Lemno, in deciding the procedure of the advance, had two dominant considerations to weigh—that progress through the difficult bush should be as rapid as possible, and that the maximum quantity of food should be obtained.

The first consideration disposed him to make use of the narrow avenues which had been beaten down in the exploration of the previous day, the second required that they should move on the broadest possible front.

Balancing their advantages, he decided that the advance should be made in five parties of 100 each, which would fan out at first, as the peninsula widened, following the curves of the beaten paths, and then converge as the land narrowed again, leaving their later formations for future decision.

Toward dawn they were heartened by the news that a supply of bows had arrived, of which fifty were to be allotted to them. Lemno allocated these equally among his troops, ten bows to each, which were put into the hands of those who were proficient in archery, or older men who had used them against the spiders before.

Plera went with Relf, who was in charge of the leftmost party. Lemno gave Jalna instructions to remain with Gleda, which was how Jalna had hoped that it might be.

CHAPTER XVI.

JALNA

LEMNO'S party advanced somewhat more rapidly than he had been able to do on the previous day. On a broader front, there were better chances of finding easier points of passage. Advance was not always quite so direct, but its greater ease was compensation for that.

And they found food. There were still nuts on some of the trees and some hard-rinded fruits on the ground, though it was not easy to see. There must be halts at times, while the grass would be combed under appropriate trees. There would be climbing and groping in tangled ground. At midday, they had all eaten enough, and some had food in their knapsacks.

At times, they would hear the squeals of disturbed pigs, and the sound of their bolting through growth too dense for them to be seen. There was no chance for a poker's thrust, or an arrow's flight, but it was good to know that they were there. They saw no spiders at all, and, so far, spirits were high, and all would have agreed that Lemno was a good leader to have.

Jalna walked beside Gleda, doing her part to break their way forward in a cheerful, casual manner, but no more than that. She seemed to take it all as a child's game rather than a matter of life and death.

Gleda was not sorry to have so light-hearted a companion, and took it more naturally than she might otherwise have done when Jalna repeatedly turned the conversation to Lemno's previous wife, and the fate she had undergone.

"Did he push it in here?" she asked, giggling, and touching the right spot.

"I was not there."

"Yes. But you must have seen—"

"Yes. I suppose he did. I expect we shall have plenty of food now, of a better kind."

"I dare say we shall. I wish he'd butchered her without sticking her first."

"But that wouldn't have been such a good idea," Gleda said reasonably.

"She'd have had a lot longer to think it over."

"I'd say you didn't like her," Gleda said.

"Like her?" Jalna echoed. Her eyes were bright with sudden hatred. "I should have liked her all right, in a good stew. You had all the fun."

Gleda's curiosity was aroused. She knew why she had hated the dead woman, but why should others feel the same way? She asked: "Why did you dislike her so much?"

Jalna began to speak, and then checked herself. The merry eyes became blank. She answered: "Oh, she just played me a trick."

Gleda realized that she was not to be taken into fuller confidence. It was Jalna who turned the conversation now. "Do you notice that there are hardly any birds in the trees—except the very small ones? I suppose the spiders must suck their eggs."

It sounded improbable, unless hunger were an extreme urge, for the largest eggs would be tiny to them; but it was a possible theory, and brought the unwelcome idea of a huge green body making a shadow above the trees, moving over them with the support of its many flexible legs, with its palpi reaching downward, feeling among the leaves.

"I saw a wood pigeon," Gleda replied, "only a moment ago."

"Yes. So did I. I wished I'd had one of the bows."

"Can you shoot?"

"Can I? Lemno'll tell you. I beat him at the last contest, and no one else could do that. Not for distance, of course."

At this point of the conversation, there was a halt while fruit was gathered. Lemno came to them. She noticed that he looked first at Jalna. He asked "You are getting on well?" That might mean anything—of the last month, or the last hour.

Jalna said: "Well enough. So you gave Destra a good dig?" Her eyes danced with delight.

He answered in the toneless way that Gleda was accustomed to hear, though it was not always used to herself: "You did not like her? Well, that can be understood."

"I should think it could."

"But you had a good husband?"

"Did I? Is a man good who is always sick?"

"But you can have another now, any hour of the day."

"Can I?" She spoke doubtfully, her eyes seeking his. Then she laughed in her merry way. "Yes, I suppose I could." Then she looked serious. "But how many men will get killed now? You shouldn't have left so many women behind."

"Perhaps not. But there were good reasons for that."

He turned away. He had not looked at Gleda, nor could she know what his thoughts had been. But she made a good guess that the trick which Destra had played had been one by which she had become his wife.

And now Destra was dead, and Jalna's husband was dead. There was no obstacle now to what might have been—no obstacle excepting herself. There was no satisfaction in that. And she saw that Jalna might make a much more attractive wife then Destra had been.

She told herself that she might overprice a danger which was not great. Even in times of famine, it was not the custom of these people to eat their wives! And for one man to do it twice! And the famine might be a passing thing.

Yet it was not quite as simple as that. She was not of these people, and she had been captured for a definite purpose, which Lemno might easily recall to the minds of his fellows. If he should disperse the thought that his experiment had not been a success, and that he would prefer another wife of his own race, would they care more to preserve her life than to share in a good meal?

Jalna said: "If many men should be killed, there may be less than one for each woman to have. They will have to have two each, or perhaps more. There will be no choice about that."

Gleda did not answer. Would she share Lemno? Even that might be preferred to the pot! Or suppose Lemno should be one of those who would not survive?

She went on in a sober mood. She heard Jalna's merry laugh at some new trifle which came to her mind, and made no reply.

CHAPTER XVII.

The Deadly Belt

LEMNO had given little attention to Jalna, and no consideration at all. His mind was on the telepathic messages which came to him from the leaders of the other columns, to which he must be continually receptive.

Yet, most of the time, these reports were negative. The finding of much or little of fallen fruit, the scuffle and squealing of pigs that fled through undergrowth that hid them from view, the absence of the dreaded spiders, the fact that Relf's leftmost column was advancing more rapidly than the others, because the ground was less difficult near the river bank—such were the reports that reached him until he heard that Relf had come to the place at which the river bank turned sharply inward, and that he must therefore halt, or swerve eastward across the front of the intermediate column, which was much farther behind.

Lemno became aware that Relf was urgently trying to reach his mind and those of the leaders of the other columns to right and left. Not knowing how far advanced they might be, his message had begun on such a note that Lemno gave instant order for all to halt, while Relf went on to explain that he had come to a point at which the bank had ceased to turn inward, and where it had been calculated that the peninsula was not more than about four miles wide. Here he should have left the river for the central point of assembly which was their objective for the first day, and where they had had no reason to suppose that there would be any difference of vegetation or terrain from those which they had been experiencing.

He reported that he had come to a narrow belt of open land, which appeared to continue across the whole breadth of the peninsula, and from which the trees appeared to have been pulled up by their roots, and smaller vegetation either trampled flat or torn out. Only a fringe of trees rose from the sloping bank of the river, which was about a hundred feet high at this point, and at the top of this wooded bank there was a solid pile of rotting debris that rose to the height of the trees. From this, great tree trunks protruded, which must have been dragged there—but by whom, and how?"

Relf's first thought had been that they had fooled themselves in assuming that the land they had abandoned had remained empty of men. Might not those from the other side of the river have moved in when they had left, or at a later time? He could not lightly suppose that this clearance had been made by anything but human hands. But then he looked toward the dark edge of the farther forest.

Great spiders moved on the forest edge, not as though they passed on their own affairs, but as though they patrolled a line which they must not leave. What could be the meaning of that?

For the moment, there was need for caution. The five parties were ordered to advance to the forest's edge, and there to halt, with care that they should not be observed, for although a spider's eight eyes are not too good beyond short distances, it can rely largely on sound and on ground vibrations. It was clear that there could be no further advance for that day. Already, shadows were long, and there was tern sky. But to cross that narrow belt of unsheltered ground? It could be done safely, Lemno presumed, in the dark hours—but that would place it in the rear when the daylight should come.

Sudden riot burst from the opposite trees.

From one spot, to which they must have been driven and herded, more than two score of frantic swine were forced out into the open. The patrolling spiders rushed, at their utmost speeds, to intercept them from gaining the farther trees, while others descended upon them in great leaps from the tops of those whose shelter they had been forced to leave.

Of the few swine which escaped the first slaughter, some attempted to bolt back to the undergrowth they had left. Two, having evaded the patrol, rushed on over the open space, toward the shelter they hoped to gain, from which they were watched by human foes that they could not guess.

After them came giant spiders that might be incapable of a sustained effort of speed, but would cover a short course at a pace that no pig could equal. One was caught almost at once. Great claws sank into its neck, and next moment the poison fang was driven in, and its squeals ceased abruptly.

The other pig had a better start. Its racing feet kept it ahead till its shoulders had entered the cover where it supposed that its safety lay. Then its frightened eyes met those of a man three feet away, whose poker was in his hand. It swerved quickly, and the movement was doubly fatal. Through the instant's pause, the claws of a pursuer were in its hams, while the poker was driven in at a different but deadlier place than it would otherwise have found.

The man gained nothing. In fact, his being in that particular spot had lost himself and his comrades the possibility of getting a good pig. The spider hauled the kicking, squealing animal back by the hams, and the next moment had reduced it to a limp weight which it settled down to devour.

The human eyes that peered fearfully out upon it saw a grass-green headless bulk, supported on eight long and very flexible legs. They saw eight eyes, in two rows of four. They saw the great bone crushers close and an aperture in the body, beneath the eyes, which was its mouth, but was no more than a toothless, tongueless, circular orifice, suck the juice from a body that continued to be crushed till it became limp and empty. It was astonishing to observe how much could be extracted in this way, how flaccid the sucked body became.

Lemno, a short distance to the right, looked out, and knew that a momentous decision must be made. The cleared space was an evidence of the work of many spiders, with an intelligence which had overcome the difficulty of getting the pigs on to open ground. He could doubtless get his little army across it during the night, when (he supposed, from what he knew of the habits of these monsters) even the patrols would be withdrawn or asleep. He could get them across—if, after what they had now seen, they would have the courage to go. But would it not be better to withdraw while no losses had been incurred?

Or should this single spider be attacked now, for which a better opportunity could not easily be imagined?

Even while he doubted, he made his plan for an attack which must be at once, if at all. Hardly conscious of the momentous decision which he had reached, he gave the order: "Follow me, and do as you see me do."

Lemno led the way out of the bushes, keeping to the rear of his antagonist. The spider could not see him, but might have become otherwise aware of his approach, for its hearing and sense of vibrations were very good. But, if it were, it was unconcerned, preferring to finish the meal it had, before prospecting for anything else which might be crawling about.

Lemno approached from behind. He saw that he had to do with a full-grown female, the most formidable of all. He walked in under her abdomen, which the length of her many-jointed legs (though they all grew from the front part of her body) raised a few feet from the ground.

Lemno held his poker ready for an upward thrust, and then waited until a dozen others were round him. "Now," he said, and all but one of his comrades were as quick as he. The pokers sank half their lengths into bowels and lungs, and the spider made a great leap, so that one or two of those beneath her were deluged by the green liquid which spurted out as the spears withdrew.

The spider did not turn. She fled in great bounds till she gained the opposite forest, and disappeared over the tree tops.

It was an encouraging event, at a time when encouragement was needed, though they could not tell whether she had been mortally hurt, or would be much the same on the next day. But Lemno thought she would die. By the next night she would have become spiders' meat. For spiders agreed with the opinion that there should be good eating in the flesh of one's own kind.

The only casualty was a stunned man, who had been kicked aside by one of the leaping legs; and Lemno must get a new poker, his having been driven in too deeply for it to come free.

The half-sucked body of the pig was dragged inward, and some ate of it, though others declined.

They lay on the forest edge until evening came, looking out upon a scene which had become quiet and vacant, except that the spiders on the farther side had resumed their patrol.

When the dusk protected them, men moved out into the open, where they made fires (for the night was chilly) and cooked what food they had, while they waited for Lemno to decide what they should do next.

CHAPTER XVIII.

JALNA WILL COME TOO

LEMNO and Gleda lay on bare ground, with no more covering than the furs they had worn during the day. (For it was only on the first occasion, when they knew that they would be returning at night, that they had gone naked through the scrub.) The night was chilly, with low clouds threatening rain. Under such conditions, it was natural to lie close for warmth. So they did, and so perhaps it was equally natural for Jalna to seek to do the same. She appeared to assume that, as Lemno had two sides, she would be welcome to one, I which Gleda did not approve. She felt that there was something here which she did not understand, but of which she had learnt enough to wish to know more.

Lemno had no objection to warmth, and when nights are cold it is well to be the centre of three. But, in fact, whatever may have been in past days, he gave Jalna no thought at all, having more important matters upon his mind.

He saw that the spiders had done work on a large scale, and they must have cooperated. They must be—or have been—very numerous to have cleared such an extent of ground. He thought of them in a new way, respect becoming a near neighbour to fear.

He was surprised also, not having supposed them capable of uniting for such a task. Yet there was little reason for such surprise. Thrown suddenly out of their natural environment, as they had been, they had to improvise or perish. And they belonged to a species which had shown adaptability, and fertility of resource, beyond parallel among earthly creatures.

The qualities which had established the spider race from Arctic and Antarctic cold to tropic heats, and from the mountain heights to the ocean depths, had not failed them now.

Yet he doubted that their adaptability would be sufficient to outwit the attacks which he was planning to make upon them, should he decide that they were not too numerous.

In the early morning, he roused Gleda, who had slept well. He said: "I have decided that I must know more before our whole force shall cross the open space, which I do not like. I shall go to see myself, while the rest will wait. You can come with me, or not, as you will."

"I will come, of course. Two will be better than one."

He looked pleased. "It is a choice," he said, "which you may have no cause to regret, should we both return."

Jalna's voice came from his other side "I will come too."

He said: "You were not asked." But then added, though in a cold voice: "Yet you may come if you will."

Gleda said nothing to that, but she was not glad. She asked: "Should we not cross the open ground before the light gets better than it is now? It is—"

"But we are not going that way. I have other plans." He rose, and left them, moving among his comrades, instructing them to withdraw into cover at once, before they should be revealed by the coming day, though he thought that to be no more than a precaution of prudence, the spiders' sight being what it was.

Yet it would have been death for the swine to have relied on that limited vision. All spiders do not weave webs, but all can spin silk, and they put it to many uses. There is one hunting spider which will lay eight radiating threads of silk in the grass, and stand in the centre of these, with a foot on the end of each, and so sensitive are they that the smallest insect will not cross a thread except at the cost of certain death. What eyes through the thick grass could be as useful as that?

These spiders had silken cords stretching the whole distance along the edge of the woods, to give them warning if any pig should bolt out, and these would have given the same warning should men have crossed them to enter the wood, but they were neglected at night, for neither spiders nor pigs will move by choice in the dark hours, and men had advantage in that. But Lemno thought that there was a safer way than that of crossing the open ground.

He arranged for Relf to take control during his absence, defending his position should the spiders make any attack, but otherwise lying close until seven days would have passed, after which, should he not have returned, he was to take complete control.

Having arranged this. Lemno went back to where he had left the two women. He said "We will eat, and then go."

When they had eaten, and were picking up weapons and other things, Jalna said: "Can I take a bow?"

Lemno said shortly: "There is one bow for every ten men. Should we put one in a woman's hands?"

"But I shoot well, as you know."

"So I do. But we are not going to fight the spiders. We go secretly, to observe."

Jalna was silenced for a moment by this, but she was persistent. She said: "But we needn't say it's for me. You have a right to take a bow, if you wish. You shoot well. A lot better than I can do."

The last remark was not true. They were both good shots, and Lemno could send an arrow farther, being so much stronger than she. But, at a moderate distance, she had a deadlier precision. It is unlikely that he was influenced by that flattery, but he saw that it was a weapon which it might be useful to have. He gave way: "We will take one for any good it may be."

Gleda watched this persistence win, and was less than pleased.

When she and Lemno were a moment apart, she asked: "Is there good reason that Jalna should come?"

"Do you mind that? Yes. She has good eyes. She can watch."

"No. Why should I? I only wondered why it should be."

He seemed to be about to say more, but then checked himself. After a moment, he smiled: "She can carry the bow."

Gleda felt more contented after that, though she would have preferred that they go alone.

CHAPTER XIX.

THE OUTSET

LEMNO led the way to the river bank, Relf walking beside him to exchange final words. Relf said: "Do you take the women far, or do they go only to bear your weapons and food for the first hours?"

"No. They will stay with me."

Relf looked his surprise. "I should have said that two of our best men—"

"Yet you might have been wrong. Had I aimed to kill spiders, it would be as you say. But I would rather have those who are soft of foot and wary of eye. Also, Jalna is very good with a bow, and Gleda has courage and wit, more than you would be likely to think."

"Then your reasons are good enough."

"They are more than I have yet said. Have you thought of the troubles they might cause among five hundred men, who will have nothing to do but feed, and wish that their own wives were here?"

"Jalna might."

"It was likely the purpose for which she came."

"Or she came for you."

"I have no doubt that she did. She has a grievance that she was disappointed before."

"When Destra told you that Jalna had wed, so that you took her?"

"So it was."

"Well, Destra is out of the way. Will you have her now?"

"I have not resolved that. But I will have her near me where she will do no mischief."

These things were said beyond the hearing of the two women, who followed behind. Relf walked with Lemno until they came down to the river bank, where he left them, and they went north-ward, keeping as near to the water's edge as the growth on the bank permitted. Bushes grew out over the water. Trees were thick on the slope above. At no great distance beyond the top of the bank, they knew that there was the piled barrier of the debris which the spiders had thrown aside. For that short distance it was unlikely that their movements would be observed. Beyond that, they did not know what they would find. Their plan could only be one of cautious advance; to be unseen, and to see.

CHAPTER XX.

THE FIRST DAY

THEY had moved for more than two hours along the foot of a bank which continued to be well wooded, and rose as they advanced, before they decided to push their way upward among the trees. Lemno, with the bow in his own hand, led the way up the bank.

As he climbed, he considered, if he should come suddenly on one of the spiders, at what part should a shaft be aimed?

An arrow may do much harm in the head. But a spider has none, and its brain is well protected with plates of bone. The eye, with most quadrupeds, is a vulnerable spot. But what if a creature have eight which work independently, though none of them may be very good?

The abdomen might be the most vulnerable, being soft on its under side, and containing lungs, heart, and bowels. But how great would the probability be that a single arrow, in such a bulk, would reach to a vital spot?

He had given Jalna his poker to carry, which she did with ease, though it was long for her. She was quick and sure in her movements, and she would have kept them light-hearted with her talk had not Lemno required silence, beyond an occasional whispered word. Gleda saw him look at Jalna more than once as though he were pleased, which was no pleasure to her, but she was careful to give no sign of this. She could wait.

When they got to the top of the bank, they found the same conditions they had observed on the previous day, except that they thought the pigs to be more numerous. The lack of earlier rain had diminished the tree crops here, as it had in their own land, though they found food enough for their own needs. That must be bad for the pigs now, and would be far worse in the winter days; already they observed much grubbing up of ground.

Still no spiders were seen, and there might be hope in that; but when Lemno considered the great extent of the land, he saw that it might mean little, and he had a fear that the cleared area might not be the last unlikely thing which they were destined to meet.

He debated in his mind whether it would be worth while to attempt to ambush a pig, or, being three, to drive it on to a poker, or to try what a shaft might do, for he was one who preferred meat to a diet of nuts or fruit, even though there should be no lack of them; which was why Gleda was with him now. But he feared the noises which they would cause. And how could a pig be cooked without the hazard of making a fire?

After a time, finding progress slow, they went back to the bank, where they could move more rapidly, though not fast. So the day went, and the next, and one more.

CHAPTER XXI.

Suspense

"IT may be forty miles to the high mountains, following the river's bends," Lemno said, "and there may be more than fifteen thousand square miles of country which have been abandoned by men, but the area which can interest us is much less than that.

"As the land rises, it becomes bare of trees. I suppose it must also be bare of food. I doubt whether there can be more than eight hundred square miles of fertile land where the swine or spiders could feed.

"We will follow the river bank for another day (and it seems that while we do that there may be little to fear), and the woods will still be dense, but not so for long. To go farther would be of little avail.

"There is one conclusion which is already beyond probable doubt. The swine breed quickly, and for many years, they have been unmolested by men. If they had had no other enemies, they would have become as numerous now as the land would support with the foods they need. There is no reason to think that starvation has kept them low, for the pig we killed was a good weight."

Neither of those who heard questioned the wisdom of this, but Gleda asked: "Then what do you mean to do?"

"We will explore the woods, crossing, if we can, the whole width of the land, and returning along the bank of the farther river. The sooner we begin that, the less the distance will be. Even now it may not take much less than the time which you said would be the limit that they should wait."

Jalna said nothing. She saw that the way of peril would become greater the longer it were deferred, but was aware of a great fear of being surrounded by monstrous foes. She would have given much at that moment to be back with the folk that they had left, and a thought passed through her mind that, if she should make an excuse to go back, there might be no opposition from them. But she saw other objections to that, and hid her fear with a jesting word, as her way was.

Lemno said: "If the spiders have set no snares into which we may fall, though they may not be meant for us, we may get through without being noticed, and shall have learned much. We know that their sight is poor, but it is the snares that we must have always to dread."

That was sense, for though all spiders do not make webs (nor, indeed, most), most of them will put the silk they weave to other uses than spinning cocoons for their eggs to hang.

There are young spiders able to spin so finely that a thread from their own small bodies would go round the earth. They will float out a thread so long and fine that, at last, it will sustain their own flight through the air, and they float away, at the wind's will, to make a home in a far place.

There are male spiders who will contrive to tie up an amorous female in silken cords (though she will be much stronger than he), so that he can copulate with some peace of mind, and have time to escape (when desire will have gone from her, and hunger remain) before she can wriggle free.

There is no possible gain to which their silk can be put which they do not try, but its most constant use is for snares and traps, about which there is little they do not know.

It might be hoped that these spiders who had grown to a huge size would spin rope-like strands, if they should use them against the pigs, so that they would be easy to see; but that was a mere guess, and it was a danger that they should keep in mind.

It was while they were looking for a good place at which to leave the river that they came to a little bay where the pigs drank.

There was no doubt of that, for there were many foot-marks in the dried mud at the water's edge. There was a narrow curve of flat land, over which the river flowed at times. Around this the bank rose, but not too sharply to be thickly wooded. The slope was most gradual at the head of the little bay, where they found a path that the pigs used. There was no sign of spiders at all.

Lemno examined this ground with care. He decided that at least thirty drank there. It would be easy to lie in ambush, and kill one, which he was tempted to do. But he was deterred, as he had been before, by the danger of lighting a fire, and by the thought of delay.

It was a better idea to use that narrow bush-sheltered passage for their departure from the river. It seemed clear that the spiders did not molest the pigs at this spot. Many of the footmarks were old;

others must have been made during recent hours. It seemed an easy road, with no cobwebs across their way. The trees ahead were too dense for the spiders to move freely beneath them. The track twisted at times, taking the easier slopes. Herbage was trodden flat, but its roof of boughs was too low for human passage without breaking of way.

Lemno went first, driving his prodder into the ground to steady himself on the slope, while he broke through the branches with his free hand, or at times hacked at one too tough to be broken, and not sufficiently supple to bend aside.

They must mount singly by such a path, but there was little for the others to do where Lemno's bulk had gone before.

So they came to the level land, to find that trees and undergrowth were just as dense, so that they would still make better progress by holding to the path that the pigs had made.

But next moment they were aware that it entered a broader aisle, where they could move with ease, and have eyes for any danger they might confront.

CHAPTER XXII.

GLEDA GOES ALONE

JALNA had been the last to climb the bank. She had the bow in her hand, and, as it became less steep, and she could see more widely ahead, she had put an arrow to the string. There was an alert prudence in that, which must be approved.

But suppose, she thought, that she should stumble, as it would be easy to do, and the shaft should go into Gleda's back?

It was so attractive a thought that there was a long moment during which Gleda's life was in peril almost as great as when she had lain with her limbs bound on her captor's floor.

Jalna did not greatly resent the thought that Lemno's wives might be more than one. She supposed that men would have to be fairly shared when the expedition should return. But to be the second of two, both by night and day? She told herself that she had no stomach for that, and she saw it to be a most likely thing. Or she might not be taken at all!

She knew that she had the reputation of having been a good wife to a sick man. She had acted both with good humour and foresight; considering that he could not last, it was a good reputation to have.

It was true that she had had no child, but what of that? A professional child-bearer of the old days might not have been made pregnant by him! She was small, but she was alert and merry, very fully alive, very certain of hand and eye. Could even Lemno equal her with a bow?

But this Gleda fought by methods which were not fair, talking to Lemno about his work in ways which she could not do. It was as though she were both woman and man. Who could stand up to that?

But suppose Lemno did not believe? She had always respected his wits, and when she thought of Destra's end she saw that she must be cautious in what she did. For he knew her skill with the bow. But was there not a way of safety in that? If she should put the arrow in with precision, where it would be certain to kill, he might doubt that the stumble had been an undesigned one. But if Gleda should be transfixed by a clumsy shot? He would not think she had meant that on purpose. And yet one which would be certain to end in death? Could she contrive that? She thought she could, and was debating where it should be done, when, for the time at least, she saw that the chance had gone.

They had come to the level ground, and the open aisle. Lemno said: "Jalna, the one who carries the bow should go first here, especially when she's the one with the best eyes. Shoot the moment you see a spider appear, without waiting to speak to us. We can dive aside as we hear the twang of the bow."

Jalna did not think much of this suggestion, but neither did she wish to give up the bow. She went two paces ahead

She asked: "Where would an arrow do the most good, if I should get the chance of a shot?"

"The eyes are the most fatal spot, but they must be hit exactly, as the bone around them is too thick to be pierced. The spider will not be blinded thereby, for each of the eight eyes has separate sight, but an arrow that goes in deeply may have a fatal effect.

"The abdomen is the softest place to attack, and the lungs and the heart are there, but a single shaft, even if it go deep, will seldom have an immediate effect."

"I suppose I could hit an eye," Jalna said confidently. "I do as well as that at the butts. But I should think the mouth would be another good place. It would be a soft way down, and even a spider would be likely to cough with an arrow there."

Lemno agreed to that. "But," he said, "It would have to be an exact shot, for the crushers around the mouth are bone which no shaft would harm."

"Well, we must see what I can do," Jalna said, her pride of art almost overcoming her fear. Here was something at which she had a skill which Gleda did not claim to possess. Lemno might have reason to see where real merit lay.

But they went on until noon, and there was no twang from the ready bow. They saw no spiders. Once or twice they heard a scurry of pigs, though they saw little of them. They found some nuts on the ground, it being evident that, even in a year of drought, the pigs were not numerous enough to clear them as fast as they fell, though in another month the nuts would probably have been eaten up.

But there might still be a great many pigs, for the nut trees were everywhere, the forests having been planted for the production of nuts and fruit, when men had ruled the land.

Lemno began to think that the defeat of the spiders might not be a difficult matter. By the time they rested at noon, though they were still alert and afraid, and chose a place where there was thick cover to which to retire, they were equally concerned that it should be one which gave them a good view, as though they were hunting spiders rather than going in fear that they would be hunted by them.

But it was almost immediately after they had started again that they came to a barrier that they could not pierce. The undergrowth before them was so dense that no light came through it at all. They hacked and struggled for a few yards, and then gave it up, and tried at what they hoped would be a better place, and so again and again, always to be confronted by the same dark, impenetrable wall.

"We might try this all afternoon, and get no farther. Why not give it up, and keep moving to the left?" Jalna asked, with more irritation than it was frequent for her to show. But, though there might be little to criticize in her physical condition (and much to admire), she was less muscular than her companions, and conscious of a strain which they did not feel.

Lemno answered: "We might go on north, of course, though not very far before we should have to turn back. If this barrier should continue, we would likely return little wiser than when we came. We must do better than that."

"Suppose," Gleda suggested, "it's a barrier to keep the pigs in? A big pig-pen, I mean. There may be hundreds on the other side."

As they talked, they stood in the gloom of the dense growth into which they had fought their way so far that it formed not only a solid wall in front, but also on either side, and a dark canopy overhead.

Lemno, looking at what he had supposed to be a great branch projecting above him, said: "That's not a branch! It's a root. It has soil clinging to it. You may be right as to what it means. But there should be an easy way to decide that. We must try a climb."

Jalna said: "I will go up!"

Gleda felt that Jalna was moving into the centre of the picture more than she was willing to permit. She said: "I can do that. I climb well."

"So can I," Jalna replied. "Lemno knows that."

Gleda said: "I suppose you can. But it would be silly for both of us to go. There would be more risk that we should be seen."

They had withdrawn into better light as this conversation proceeded, and Lemno looked at them with more understanding than he permitted himself to show. He said to Gleda: "It may be dangerous to go really high. Would you die there, or live on the ground?"

"I dare say I shall do well enough. I am quick in the trees."

"Well, as you prefer. Jalna has the bow."

That was a cryptic remark, to which Jalna might have replied that it would be simple to lay it down; but they both understood that it had been decided that Gleda was to go, and that there would be no profit in further words.

Jalna found some consolation in the thought that it really might be a dangerous thing to do, which she had not considered before. Suppose they were to watch Gleda being caught in the tree tops by a monstrous arm, and have her sucked-out body dropped at their feet? Even spiders may be beneficial at times, and Jalna saw that it would not be easy to think of a way in which one of them would be better employed.

Gleda walked a few paces forward, choosing her tree, with the others moving behind.

Jalna exclaimed sharply: "Look at this!" She bent down to what seemed to be the entrance to a tunnel, low and dark. She said: "I can see light. It must be a passage the pigs have made."

They all looked. There was a distant point of light, the significance of which was beyond doubt. Gleda said: "It doesn't really prove that we were wrong about the pigs, but it shows the barrier's not very thick."

Lemno said: "It means it's unlikely that the pigs are more numerous on that side than they are here. But you'd better get up, and see all you can, so that you don't risk too much."

Gleda felt in better spirits than at any time since she first considered Jalna a serious rival for her precarious position as Lemno's wife. She had asserted herself successfully, and she knew that she climbed well.

Those who watched her as she went up were of the same opinion on that point. Climbing was a form of athletics which they all understood. It was practiced from childhood. It was not the mere capacity to get to the top of a difficult tree by which it was judged, but by accuracy in choosing the best ascent, and by the certainty and speed with which the ascent was made—above all, by the speed.

And Lemno, watching one whom he had not seen in a tree before, and who had not learned the art in his own land, became well content. He had seen the speed with which the spiders moved over the tree tops. He could guess how rapidly they would descend anywhere that the branches would allow—anywhere that the trees were not too close, or were unequal in height, and he knew that Gleda must seek a place where she could see far, which would not be where branches were thick and close.

They watched her swift ascent till the leaves hid her. They heard her movement for a further moment, and then she was gone.

CHAPTER XXIII.

GLEDA DOES NOT RETURN

JALNA did not make the mistake of depreciating what they had both seen to be expertly done. She was too quick-witted for that. She said: "She went up like a squirrel." She asked a moment later: "How shall we get on when the leaves fall?"

Lemno looked at her with approval of a quality which he had observed in her before. She would so often give voice to his own thought. He saw that this was partly because she chattered, which he certainly did not. But he saw also that it was because she was alert and nimble of mind. He had a passing thought that, if women were not so jealous, there would be some good points in a ménage of three. Why could they not, in a sensible way—? He said: "Yes. They are just beginning to fall. It would be a disadvantage for us. But we shall have time enough—either to kill or to die."

After a time he said: "She should be back now." But another half-hour passed after that, while they sat waiting, with only occasional words, their ears being alert for any sound which might be evil or good; and they took such confidence as they could from the fact that they heard nothing at all.

They looked at the little heap of encumbrances which she had left, with thoughts to which neither of them would have cared to give words.

Jalna looked at the fur cloak, and a hope rose. It would be so much warmer than the fibre tunic she wore. And it must surely become hers in the end. And would not that in itself be very near to a declaration that she had won the place which she had some reason to hope that Gleda vacated now?

She looked up at the tree beneath which they camped—the one Gleda had run up "like a squirrel" a few hours before—and she had a new fear. She asked: "Are we safe here?"

"The dusk is coming," Lemno replied, "and we shall be safe here till the dawn. No one has known a spider to hunt in the night. In the day, it would not be a place at which to remain. I suppose we could be in the bushes before one could scramble to the ground. But I would not say we could get too far for an arm to follow, and twitch one of us out by the leg."

It was a picture which he made too vivid for her comfort, and it was with a trembling voice that she replied: "Well, I suppose we shall wake in time. A half-grown one—"

"Yes. So it could. But we need not concern ourselves about that. It is Gleda's coming down I would like to hear."

Jalna saw that it would not be a good time for saying more of her own fears. She said no more, and they lay down together, the chill of the night being good reason for her to lie close to one who showed no awareness of her, having other matters upon his mind.

It was not only the question of Gleda's safety. He saw that he could not afford the time for patient waiting. Unless there should be further progress at once, either forward, or by returning the way they had come, he would be later than the limit of time which he had set, and Relf might decide to abandon the enterprise, and follow those who had gone over the farther river. It would be a most probable course for him to take.

To go back with a tale of failure would be no worse than to remain undecided there. He did not know what might be beyond the impeding barrier, but the fact that Gleda had disappeared in that soundless way suggested a trap, into which whoever might follow would fall in the same way.

He might send Jalna up (but would she go?), and abandon the enterprise if she should disappear in the same manner. But he did not like the idea. It would be ignominious to return with so blank a tale.

They might go on northward when day should come, leaving the barrier on their right, and there might be a limit to its extent. But even for this dubious plan, the remaining time should not be long. Apart from that, he had a strong reluctance to leaving the place to which Gleda, were she still alive and free, would surely return. What would she do, if she should be unable to find them, and know nothing of where they had gone? Could he leave her a written word? He realized that he was not even sure that she could read, though there might be a little doubt about that. But to read his script, in his tongue? There was more doubt there, though he thought he could make it plain.

After a time, he gave Jalna a nudge: "Are you awake?"

"Yes," she replied quickly, with a short catch in her breath.

"Would you go to find what Gleda has done wrong, when the light allows?"

She was silent for a moment, after which he laughed: "It is not that which I shall ask you to do. Will you stay here alone for one day, after which, if I do not return, you will go back by the way you came, and tell our friends that there is no more to be done?"

"Why should you go, when she has shown that it is foolish to do so? I should say that we had better wait together here for that length of time, and then return when we are sure that she has come to a bad end."

"But I did not ask you what we should do. I asked whether I could rely on you to do as I say."

"I would do it for you; though, if I am to be left alone, I shall be greatly afraid. I shall hide under the boughs during the day, so that you will have to be here before I shall be seen at all."

"I should expect that."

"Is there food enough, so that I need not seek it at a great risk?"

"There will be enough if I leave you all that I have, and you take that which Gleda has ceased to need. It is water which you will need."

"Well, I will do it. You will be pleased?"

Lemno understood that she sought praise, or perhaps more than that, which would imply some promise for future days. He saw also that it might be important that she should not fail to remain for the time he had said. He judged that, when she should be left alone, it would not be many hours before she would turn her eyes to the backward path. He asked: "Have you known of a debt which I did not pay?"

"No," she replied. "I shall trust you with a quiet mind. What shall I do with Gleda's fur, if she should not return?"

He saw, from point to point, the way that her mind had moved, but there could be only one answer to that. He said: "Well, it would be foolish to leave it here."

His mind reverted to Gleda, and a new thought came that she might return by some other way and that some message should be left. But he had nothing on which to write. Well, if Jalna would be there for another twenty-four hours—

His mind wandered again, for the recollection that he had nothing on which to write brought back a mystery of the historical period with which he had been dealing, which had baffled his imagination. He had come on statistics of the destruction of forests which took place to produce paper on which news could be printed for distribu-

tion, and the figures had seemed to him to be so inexplicable, so incredible, that he had hesitated as to whether he should retain these
records as authentic or destroy them, as being of such blatant inac-
curacy as to be unworthy of preservation.

He saw, clearly enough, that the absence of telepathic communication required some alternative method of distributing information more generally and more quickly than could be done by the
medium of the printed book. But the figures upon which he had
come told of so many thousands of acres of forest trees destroyed
every day to supply material for these newspapers, that he had been
baffled. This was, he recalled, a time at which men were said to be
so short of timber that they could not build enough houses in which
to live.

It was not a subject on which he would have spoken to anyone
up to a week ago. But Gleda had shown a receptivity and response
to such conversations which had been both gratifying and stimulat-
ing. So from this new habit, he said something to Jalna concerning
that which was an enigma to him, and when he thought he had made
it clear, she answered, with the kind of giggle which she felt would
gratify him: "You mean they used to write things on trees? How
funny they must have been!"

She knew that all men have a childish inclination to concern
themselves with things that do not matter at all (which is why
women possess the earth), and that to humour their weaknesses will
make them complaisant in issues which really do. She would have
been astonished to know how much she had fallen in Lemno's es-
teem as she made that giggling reply—astonished, but not dismayed,
for she knew that there are more effectual weapons with which
women can fight, and she thought herself more proficient in them
than Gleda would ever be. Besides, where was Gleda now?

CHAPTER XXIV.

Gleda's Return

LEMNO was asleep now, for the anxieties of his mind were overcome by fatigue.

After a time, a half moon showed overhead. The strip of visible sky was so narrow that its dim light must be quickly gone, but, for a few minutes, it would shine directly down upon them, so that Jalna—who lay awake busy with her more personal problems, and fearful of every movement that stirred in the forest night—could see Lemno's fur wrapped form at her side, and the out-thrusting branches above; and then she became aware of a rustling sound overhead. "Lemno! There's something coming down through the trees!" She picked up the bow.

Lemno, waking, took it from her. A sudden hope rose. "We shall not shoot," he said, "till we know."

The noise came again, lower than before. Certainly, something was descending the tree.

Lemno said: "Get under cover quickly." He stood up himself. His poker lay at his feet. He had an arrow upon the cord. He was equally ready for greeting or strife.

From thirty feet overhead, something crashed down through the snapping boughs, into the bushes at their left hand. Lemno dropped the bow. He moved fearlessly toward the place where the body fell, though he picked up the poker first. He called: "Gleda, is that you? Are you hurt?"

A quavering voice, unlike anything which he had heard from Gleda before, answered: "I cannot tell. I cannot move for the thorns."

He moved forward, throwing off his fur, and indifferent to the brambles which tore a hundred scratches on naked skin. Gleda felt strong arms lifting her from the bed of thorns which had been flattened by the impact of her fall, but not enough so for her to have

90

been broken or bruised by the solid ground. He said: "Thunder! But you are cold. I should not have thought you would slip like that."

"My hands were too numb."

"What happened? Are you all right now?"

"If I were warm! And could have something to eat."

He postponed asking more until he had given her water (which had become their more acute problem) from his flask. While she ate and drank, she lay in her own fur, with his spread above it for extra warmth. By this time the direct light of the moon had gone, and she could be felt rather than seen. He drew her closer. He asked: "Tell me what the trouble has been?" But she did not reply, and he realized that she was asleep.

Well, nothing could be better than that. But he had a lively curiosity as to what she would tell when she waked—and would she be fit to move when the light should come?

CHAPTER XXV.

WHAT GLEDA SAW

WITH no logical reason, Jalna's fears left her after Gleda's re-turn, as though the climax of the event had come, and there could be nothing further to dread. But she did not sleep as quickly as those who lay beside her. Gleda's brief absence had given her expectation, where before there had been nothing more than an old desire, and a vague hope.

Now she was more than disappointed. She saw that Gleda meant much more to Lemno than she ever would.

"Yet," she thought, "there are ways—and ways. Am I to be thwarted a second time?" She hoped her wits would be sufficient to bring her to something better than that.

But she slept at last, and so heavily that even her fear of de-scending spiders did not rouse her when daylight came. But Lemno's voice was urgent: "Jalna, you must find food. I will stay here for a while. I do not want Gleda to waken yet."

It was a mission she did not like, and she guessed that Lemno's motive was not as simple as were his words, but she found no ex-cuse. And it was a fact that Gleda lay with a look of exhaustion upon her face which sleep could not disguise.

Jalna said, with more sulkiness than she often showed: "Very well. But I shall not go far. I should not like to be lost."

As she passed out of hearing, Lemno drew the fur away, and looked at Gleda's sleeping form, which was reddened with many scratches, and streaked with dried blood. He saw a large thorn over her knee which must have been an inch deep in the flesh. "She must have been worn out, indeed, not to feel that," he thought, "but when she wakes, as she will, she may be glad to know it is not there."

So he pulled it out, with a sharp wrench, at which a spurt of blood followed, and she waked, with a cry of pain. But her expres-sion changed at once when their eyes met.

He looked at the thorn as he said: "I thought you might like to have it out when you waked."

"Yes." She tried to rise, and sank back. Pains were too numerous and complicated to be ignored. Movement must be experimental at first. She said with distaste: "What a mess I am!"

"If there's nothing worse than scratches—"

"Help me up, and we'll soon know."

As she rose, she disclosed a livid bruise on her left side, of such an area as caused Lemno to feel her ribs, so that she would have found it easy to scream with pain; but he said they seemed to be all of one piece, and being assured of that, she said: "You must want to know what I saw, and why I was so long away, more than how many ribs I've got left. Well, I'd better begin."

"I should be glad to hear it before Jalna gets back. She's hunting round for our breakfast now."

Gleda sat down with some natural deliberation, and went on: "I got up to the tree tops without difficulty. There was nothing in that. And then I saw a great green dome in front of me, higher than the trees. I got as near to it as I could, and was about at the top of its circular vertical wall, where the dome began, and quite close. What we have come up against is the debris which must have been piled up when the ground was cleared. This has been packed tightly, and the building was close enough to it for the upper branches to about touch the wall. The place was built of great cords of green silk, which the spiders must have woven and then twisted into walls, and a domed roof.

"But before that, I had decided to climb up to the top of the dome. I don't say it was wise, but that's what I did. I balanced out on a branch as far I could, and then had no more than a six-foot jump to get on to it, where the wall ended, and the curve of the dome began.

"It was as easy to get up as it could be. I just dug my toes in between the ropes of silk, which were horizontally woven, and walked up, without even using my hands after a time, as the curve of the dome increased. If there had been any danger, I could have slipped down, and got back among the trees, in about twenty seconds. But I could see nothing, and I suppose nothing saw me, until I'd reached the top of the dome, and then I looked down on about the strangest sight that I've ever seen.

"There was a fresh space being cleared, and the spiders were dragging great trees out by the roots with ropes of silk (they must have been made of that), four or five of them pulling together. It made me realize how much greater strength these beasts have than any animal of the same size, and as to the ropes, I suppose that thickness of twisted silk would—"

"Why didn't you come back? It sounds as though you could have done so quite safely then."

"So I could; and perhaps I should have. But it seemed to me that I hadn't got much that was worth telling while I didn't know what the inside of that building was like, and couldn't tell what it was for. But I didn't see that I was running any great risk. I went back into the trees, and worked round till I was at the north side of the dome, and looking down from there I could see a porch—what looked like a door—on that side, facing the forest. So I went down there, keeping well back among the trees, and then wriggling through the undergrowth till I could look out opposite the door, which is what it was, or at least an archway. I didn't see any way that it closed, and don't think it did. Seeing what's inside, I don't see why it should."

"What was inside?"

"I'm coming to that. It was still quite quiet, and I thought I needn't go half a dozen yards from the trees to look into that doorway, and I knew it ought to be done. I suppose I'd made up my mind to do it, but I was afraid all the same. Telling myself that the longer I watched and nothing happened the safer it must prove to be, I waited, wiping the blood of where I'd been scratched, to pass the time."

"You got these scratches there?"

"I got some. I wasn't like I am now. You can't wriggle through thorn bushes with no clothes on, and not get a few marks. I didn't mind about them.

"I got up at last, and walked out from the trees. The space between them and the doorway was just about as much as a spider needs. It didn't look that much, but it was. I learned that before long.

"I stepped quickly across that bare space, seeing a thin silk rope on the ground, and stepping over it without giving it half a thought, and I looked into a great empty space that was almost dark. At least, I thought it was empty till I looked up at the roof and saw that there were about thirty dead spiders hanging up there. They were all upside down, hanging by their legs, which were bunched together, and with a cord to hold up their abdomens, as there were no legs on them."

"You didn't look long?"

"No. But why do you think that?"

"Because you've got quite a wrong idea. What did you think it meant?"

"I thought spiders must be as bad as men."

"As bad as—Oh! I see what you mean. Well, they are. I believe the female eats the male when she's finished with him for other purposes, about as often as not. But those spiders weren't hung up in a larder. They weren't dead. And they weren't keeping still—as you'd have seen if you'd given them a second look. They were just moulting their skin and bones, and they must have been working their legs, on and off, the whole time, because that's how they make the skin split. I don't know why they've made themselves a shelter for that, but I suppose, with the size they are, they haven't found as many well-sheltered corners as they require. The amazing thing is the way they've learned to work together, since they found it necessary for their own lives. The spider has always been the most adaptable of created things, but they've always been so independent—so individualistic—that most of them haven't even been able to endure family life. But what I want to know is what happened to you."

"That was when it did. I thought I heard a noise. I feel sure I did, though I don't know what it was, and nothing came of it which made any difference to me. But I bolted back. You can't blame me for that."

"It may have been no more than the splitting of one of their skins."

"I believe it was. It sounds quite a likely explanation. It was that sort of noise. But I didn't stand thinking it out then. I just ran. And I was in too much hurry to step over that silk cord on the ground. And the moment my foot touched it—the very moment—a great spider came rushing along that narrow space between the building and the forest. I should say it took him five seconds to reach the place where I had been standing, and I'd got into the bushes in about four. His arm came in after me, and that's how I got this bruise."

"I don't understand that. It doesn't look the way that a spider's palpi would strike you. It wouldn't give a flat bruise."

"What a lot you know! It didn't happen like that. It caught its claw in a branch, and it was the branch which struck me. I suppose the way it happened saved my life, in a way. I was too frightened to feel it then, but it must have knocked the breath out of me, so that I couldn't climb. I just grovelled and wriggled on, and then I must have fainted when I felt safe.

"It was dusk when I became conscious enough to think I ought to get back to you, and I climbed up to the tree tops, where I could cross to this side, and I could only do it very slowly, and by then it was dark, and I found coming down, as I was, harder than going up, and I wondered whether I could keep awake, and hold on, till the light should come. And then the moon rose, and I thought I'd try to come down. I was so cold by then that—but at last I did. You know how I did that."

"You were from moonrise coming down that tree?"

"Not coming down. It was coming through the trees. And then I daren't move till the moon shone straight down."

"You didn't do badly," Jalna's voice came from behind them. "But oh! what a sight you are. Oh yes. I've heard most of it. You were too occupied with yourselves to take any notice of me. And I've got nuts enough to last us through the day."

Lemno looked at Jalna, and was not pleased. But he had no answer to the merriment in her eyes. He knew she must have returned on quiet feet, but he knew also that he should have been more watchful in that open place, now that the light had come.

Besides that, an idea had come to him while he had been talking, for which Jalna would be of use. He had no mind to quarrel with her. He said: "We will eat; and we may drink with less stint; for we are not going to cross the land."

CHAPTER XXVI.

A Part for Jalna

LEMNO said: "We cannot go farther across the land, as we had intended, because, however you might try"—he looked at Gleda—"our progress would be too slow. We should not be back in the time agreed, and the others might have gone.

"Besides that, we have learned enough.

"We cannot all return the way we came: we should be too late. One must go, and two must stay here. It will be best for you, Jalna, to go, taking the message which I shall send."

"I am to go alone?" Her voice was frightened and rebellious. She looked at Gleda, and there was no love in her eyes.

"It is not much to do," he went on. "You know the way, which is safe. The danger will be greater for those who stay."

"I wonder! What message would you like me to take?"

"You will tell Relf from me to bring here every man who can use poker or bow. It should be timed so that they will be here before noon, so that the men will not have travelled far on the last day, as there is no room for five hundred to camp, and not be observed. I must have the men fresh (for I shall attack the spiders at once), and the hours of daylight which we shall need."

Jalna looked at him with eyes which were merry and bold. "Why should I do this great thing? It is what a man might ask of his wife."

"You are one of us, and each, woman or man, should do all he can."

"But I may have resolved that I have had more than enough. Should I get back alive, I may go on to the farther land."

"So you can, if you will. But a message may first be said. You may take the bow."

"I shall sleep cold, being alone. Do I take a fur?"

Their eyes met in a conflict of wills which was clear to Gleda, although the one had a merry, mischievous look, and the other was cold and calm. There was a moment of silence, and then Lemno said: "That's fair. In time of war, many rules may be set aside." He loosed the thong from his own neck, and threw the fur over her shoulders, where it hung with more than a foot trailing the ground. "Is it agreed now? Can you move with speed, being so cumbered throughout the day?"

Jalna saw that she had gained much, though not precisely what she had hoped. Yet to try for more might be to lose all. She said: "It is agreed. I can manage it…though a smaller one would be better."

Gleda saw what must be done. She said: "You can have mine, rather than that." She looked at Lemno, to see how he would take such an offer from her.

He said: "It is clearly the better way."

So it was. Better for all. Jalna still had an outsize garment, which she must bear over her shoulder during the day, but it was much less in weight and length than Lemno's, and Lemno would have one of the right length, which would be better for two in the night. Yet it left Gleda bare during the day, for Jalna's tunic would have been useless for her.

Lemno said: "Will you go now? Will you go with speed?"

Jalna laughed: "I am gone now."

She turned as she spoke, and in a moment was out of sight.

Lemno looked at Gleda, still beside him but now naked. He asked: "You are ill-pleased?"

She did not profess to think that he had meant less than he did. She answered: "I don't mind. It was the only way."

"There will be much gossip."

And so there would. The fur was a mark of rank which only one like himself, or one of their wives, should wear. Jalna would not need to assert. It would be concluded at once that she had replaced Gleda, or, at least, been put at her side.

Lemno added, in the toneless voice which Gleda was used to hearing: "You react well." Then he said: "No. Were you less hurt than you are, I would put you to better use while we wait here."

She was still angry at what had been done, and at what it might mean in the future days, but slowly she smiled. "I may be less hurt than I look."

He smiled then too. "Do you think that?"

She made a motion which he could not mistake.

Jalna, going a burdened way, had the worse of the next hour.

CHAPTER XXVII.

LEMNO IS AFRAID

LEMNO said: "If we take this land—as I think we may—I shall be a great name. It is of that I am most afraid."

"Why? You could do much."

"I am afraid lest I might do more than I should."

"If you see the pit, you can walk aside."

He became silent on that reply, and their thoughts went forward by different ways.

They had been together for two days when they waked at dawn, and this conversation began. They had had no occupation except to talk while they lay side by side, for she had become aware of an injured rib when she had sported too rashly two days before. He had only left her since then to forage, and their minds had gone far toward such harmony as their bodies already knew.

Now her thoughts turned to Jalna, whom she had ceased to fear, but not to recognize as a factor with which she would have to deal in the coming days. As he remained silent, she made a direct attack on this issue. "If you are king of this land, you will need more than one wife."

"Why?"

"Well, you will. If there should be many deaths, there must be many women unwed, which it could not be expected that a king would allow."

He had read too much history to question that. Cruelty or vice had been the alternative evils of monogamous lands, whenever men had become fewer than women.

She added, as he was slow to reply: "You might find Jalna useful for that."

He looked surprised. "You would not mind?"

"Not if you would tell her one thing, so that she would be very sure not to forget."

"What is that?"

"That you would wring her neck if anything should happen to me."

"You think that?"

"Should you call me a fool?"

"Well, we will see." She thought he was amused.

This exchange had diverted him from the problem which had been disturbing his own mind, but he resumed it as he said: "We have broken loose from the corrupt dominion of law, thinking that we were civilized enough to endure freedom without wrecking our civilization. But, if authority should become mine, I might be greatly tempted to make controls."

"I don't see why you should. I suppose that telepathic decisions would still be made. You could still rule by the clear mind and the strong will, as you have done before now."

"So we hope it would be."

"Besides that," she went on, thinking that he vexed himself with small cause, "It is not personal tyranny that has ever greatly troubled the world. One tyrant cannot do much to obstruct its ways, especially if men see him for what he is. The tyrant will always wish to be praised, and he will be dead before long. It is when people are duped to think that they govern themselves—it is when they tell themselves they are free, while every day gives them a new chain, or tightens one they have worn before—it is then that they come to wreck."

He looked at her speculatively. "You talk as one who knows much."

"I am learning from you."

"Is it only that?"

"Will you say what else it could be?"

"I will say that my canoe took a good voyage."

"Yes. You may say that. And you may say it was handled well."

"A man will do much for his own life. I think we may be content. Yet there is one thing I regret. I would be back at my own work, rather than here."

"Was it so much to you as that?"

"It was a tale that was never done. And I was interrupted at a crisis of human fate of which the issue was hard to see."

"With all your knowledge of earlier days, could you not deduce what it would be?"

"No. For though the history of man is always the same, it is always the same in a different way. At the time to which I have come there were two tyrannies dividing the world, which were afraid, and yet preparing to clash. And they were both insecure, so that they might be overthrown from within before they would feel the impact of outer foes."

"Were these tyrannies equally bad?"

"I would not say that. They were hard to compare. In some aspects they were strangely alike, reaching to the same place by moving in opposite ways. Extremes met. There was much self-delusion with both. They were both deluded by their rulers to a degree which made large proportions willing, or even eager, for their own degradation. You may say that they were going downhill on most willing feet. There was a difference in the ruthlessness of one, in which opposition was stamped out with torture and death: it was the more virulent and aggressive. Yet it might be a valid contention that those among them who were not opposed to their chains found them to be looser than those which were worn in more western lands.

"Under both systems, great exertions were made by their masters to convince them that they moved of their own wills; and it was only when they broke the rank that the whip fell.

"They were also curiously alike in that they appealed successfully rather to the baser than the nobler instincts of men. The western system bought the support of large sections of the community by taxing the whole country for their particular benefits, and then of others by promising that they should be favoured in the same way. It was not generally observed that when this had been completely done they would all be back where they were before, or worse, owing to the number of officials they would have to support. And that has to be qualified by the fact that these benefits went to sections of the community which were well organized, and could give large sums of money and great blocks of votes to those who gave favours to them. There was always a large disorganized part of the population, all of whom could be advantageously plundered, and many of whom could be successfully fooled.

"There were still laws punishing theft. If a poor man took the property of one who was rich, he would be punished in merciless ways, but if a combination of poor men should make a law taking the property of a minority which were richer than they, they would have done nothing wrong, because it was implicitly held that minorities had no rights. There was nothing that could not be justified if it were done in the name and the form of law.

"Equity in taxation must always have been difficult to attain, but in the twentieth century of the Christian era, as it was then called, it was not attempted at all. A budget-making politician would talk of expediency as his only and natural goal, and even his opponents would not think to protest against that which was done by all.

"At the time with which I have been concerned, the worship of numerical majorities was teaching that comfort and security could be attained by the simple process of making a law that everyone should be comfortable and secure, and that everyone should seek to profit by the labour of others rather than by exerting himself. This was undermining the foundations of liberty in the western world, and weakening its resistance to the more implacable serfdom of eastern lands. But it remained to be seen what, if it were tested, the ultimate power of that resistance would prove to be.

"In comparing these slave systems of east and west, there is another difference which it is fair to recognize, beyond the fact that they were arriving at the same goals, the one by direct violence and the other by confiscatory laws, in that the western states could at any time have recovered freedom and honour had an actual majority, whether bribed or not, united for that purpose, while those of the east must face torture or death, as large numbers did, to the admiration (but without the help) of the western world.

"There were other resemblances, and fine distinctions, which have been fascinating to study, though it can be little pleasure to you to hear me summarize them. I have already been too loquacious."

"As to that," Gleda laughed, "you may observe that you have not sent me to sleep. I must hope that you will resume your work when the last spider is dead. I am most curious to know what the end of the tale will be."

"There can be no end while our kind endures. You will only learn of the chapters which intervene until we come to the one we are writing now. But it is strange that you should care so much for the dead time, not having studied it in the same way."

"Well, it just happens I am. You will not blame me for that?"

"No. If I can believe—"

"You can," she said, and was silent.

Could she say more? Could she tell him a most incredible thing? She could see advantages if he should believe, confusions if he should not. If he should be unsure, it might be the worst of all. On the whole, she thought not.

CHAPTER XXVIII.

Jalna Has Done Well

JALNA came through the trees. She had the bow in her hand. She wore the fur, which she had stitched up to her own length. It was ragged. Her eyes were bright, and her tongue ready to boast. She knew that she had done well, and had no doubt that Lemno would approve. She hoped that Gleda would not be pleased.

She asked: "I have not been long? Relf will be here in two days, or perhaps less. He has had difficulties about food, and the men were scattered, combing the land. I have only five arrows now. I have killed a spider with one."

"*Killed* a spider?" Lemno asked, with incredulity in his voice.

"Yes. I am sure of that. The arrow went in at one of her eyes. It was a big she. It went in almost all its length. It's gone down the river now."

"You say the arrow's gone down the river?"

"No. The spider, of course." Jalna's eyes were alight with merriment. Laughter hindered her words.

"I thought she'd got me when she came down over the trees on the river bank. They weren't very thick just there. And the rate she came at! And the way she pushed down between branches where you wouldn't believe! They were the *beastliest* eyes! And I knew she thought she'd got me, as sure as sure. I didn't miss by an inch, with her arms almost touching me as I shot. I said 'Don't you believe it. I'm not for you,' and shot her through the lower left eye nearest the fang on that side.

"There was only the feathered end of the shaft left sticking out. I had only a second to look at that, and then she fell sideways along the slope of the trees. She turned over, and went out of sight. And then I heard a great splash, and when I got down to the water I could see her floating away.

"She seemed to be struggling not to be turned upside down, but there wasn't much she could do about that. She was getting quieter as she went out of sight. I should think she went over the falls a few hours ago."

Neither of those who listened doubted her tale. It was too clearly told, the note of triumph too authentic for that.

Lemno said: "It was coolly done. I must make you captain of those who handle the bows."

It could have been said as a jest, but she knew that it was genuine praise. "And now," he added, "will you tell me more of what Relf said?"

"That's not much. I told him I didn't think there'd be room by the river here for all those men to lie hidden for many hours, even if they could get food, without being seen. So I thought you meant to attack at once.

"So he's bringing the best men first. Those with the bows and men with good pokers and knives. The others won't be held back, but he says you'll understand that they can only come in a thin line, as they'll have to keep to the bank."

"They'll come faster as it gets trampled down."

"It's a bit that way already," Jalna replied cheerfully. But the words, and the tale of triumph she had just told, brought an anxious doubt to his mind. How long would it remain secret? Could he even be sure it was secret now?

Was it merely by chance that a spider had discovered Jalna? Fortunately, it was dead. And the spider is the least gregarious of creatures. Normally, it cannot even endure family life, and must always go its own way. But he had seen how far they had modified this custom under the pressure of economic law. Was it chance alone which had led that spider to watch the trees under which Jalna had made her silent and furtive way?

"And," Jalna was going on, "he said no one was to come with less than two days' food after they arrived here, and three would be much better than that. He said, if there is to be a big fight before we can get moving from here, a lot of starving men wouldn't be much use to you."

Lemno saw sense in this, though it conflicted with the plan he had made, which had been both to alarm the spiders and to draw them together for what he hoped might be a decisive struggle, for which he would need every man who would have a poker to push.

He thought, as he had done many times before, that the compromise which had divided strength might have fatal consequences both for his own party, and the larger one which had gone into

Gleda's land. But he knew that the majority had anticipated that he would fail, and that a flying remnant would soon be added to them. Well, if he should win tomorrow's battle, it would be a different matter.

It was no more than midday when Relf came. After him came a continuous procession of men in single file bearing nothing but weapons in their hands, and knapsacks on their backs for food. Those who were fortunate had a portion of cooked pork. None had much. They had been unmolested and the only spider that they had seen had been one in the river. They had been heartened by that, though, when they were told how it had died, they could not have much hope that others would perish in the same way. It was not only that it must be a most skilful shot. It was one which could only be taken directly facing a spider at a short distance, so that to fail would be death. The bowmen heard of it, and began to talk of other parts of a spider's anatomy which, they were willing to think, would be as vulnerable, and could be hit from ambush.

Relf said to Lemno: "The men will soon be cramped here, and if they scatter they will not be easy to draw together without noise being made. Will you tell me the plan you have?"

"Yes. It is simple, and requires only that you should lead them by the way that Gleda has found, leaving the place that the spiders have built on your right hand, and going on to line the wood at the side of the ground they are clearing now.

"I shall set fire to the building, which may cause them to assemble to see what has occurred; we will attack the others while they are confused by the fire. Do you call it a good plan?"

"I have no better of which to talk. Do you think the building will burn?"

"Yes. I should say it will burn well. You should be cautious till you see the blaze, as you must depend upon that to distract the spiders while you take up positions to do them the most harm you can. Have you got arrows?"

"Each man carries twelve, and we have twice that number in reserve."

"Good." He told what Jalna had done, which Relf praised. He turned to her to say: "You must come with us, to give courage to others, and to show your skill."

Jalna laughed. "I am to shoot spiders' eyes when they are about five seconds away? I should be dead in the next hour. You must ask me something better than that."

Relf saw the point. Yet all must do what they could, and he did not regard her life as of more value than those of others who might die in the next hour. But he said only: "You have great skill with the bow."

Jalna liked to be praised. She would be glad to be known by all as having done some spectacular deed *if* she could feel a reasonable confidence that she would survive to enjoy reward. She said: "You cannot shoot all your spiders in the eye. It is a small mark, and they must be exactly opposite for the shaft to go in as it should. But we ought to know what *is* the best place to choose. If you like, I will do this: put me in a position where I could not be reached, and I will shoot arrows into any places you say, so that you will know what is best for the bowmen to do."

She had a cold fear in her heart the moment after she said this, for it brought a vision of many spiders at which she must shoot in a short time; and how could any such position be safe?

But she had said it now, and Relf was replying: "It is a good thought, for there are few who could make such tests as well as you. We will see."

He thought also that it would give better heart to the bowmen, some of whom were now advancing on shaky legs, if it were known that a girl would test the spiders in this way—and one who had already sent one to death, as they had seen when its body blundered among the rocks, with some of its great legs in the air.

Gleda also looked at Jalna with approval, for though she could not call her a friend, she felt that it was a brave offer to make. She said generously: "It is more than most would have either courage or skill to do."

Jalna looked at Gleda, as she said that, and an idea came to her mind. Why should she be risked, and Gleda remain in a safe place? She said: "Oh, but I am greatly afraid! I have not your coolness when danger comes. But were you with me, I should not tremble at all. They say they will put me in a safe place, so that there will be no danger to us. It is just that I feel secure when you are near, who are so much cooler than I."

Relf, who was never patient with the illogical process of a woman's mind, said shortly: "Well, it was your own offer. Did you mean it, or not?"

"It is how I say. If Gleda will be near, I shall not be too much afraid to draw the cord with a steady hand."

Relf considered that she had done this once already when no other woman was near, and in another moment, he might have said so, but Gleda was quicker than he. "I cannot see how I could be of much help, but if that be how you feel, I will not refuse."

Jalna said: "Well, I always hate being alone."

106

Gleda was fair enough to admit to her own mind that there might be some truth in that. But she also wondered: "Does she think, if we should both be in a spider's power, that she might escape alone?"

CHAPTER XXIX.

BATTLE!

LEMNO toiled with impatient energy, setting the pace for the little group to right and left who worked with him to break through the debris barrier, and fire the building from the side at which their activities would be least likely to be observed. He had no reason to doubt that he had made a good plan, nor that he was where he should be.

But the work was taking far longer than he had expected, and he had no doubt that the attacking force had taken up its positions some time ago, and would already be watching impatiently for smoke to rise over the dome.

But the barrier was pierced at last, through his own toil and the example he set, and dry wood, which had been gathered by others, was dragged through the tunnel and piled against the side of the great building, and set afire.

Lemno need not have doubted that it would burn well. As the bonfire crackled alight, an arm of flame shot up the outside of the wall, and next instant was spreading upon the dome. It spread sideways also, and in three minutes its surrounding arms met on the farther side, so that the whole building was a circular furnace.

Lemno had planned to go round the building to join his comrades before it should be completely alight, but he had underestimated the fury with which such a building would burn. He got clear with two others behind him; but those who followed were driven by the heat into the shelter of the bush, and must proceed at the best pace they could make, with the branches igniting above their heads.

With the fire at his back, and a bow in his hand, Lemno gazed on a scene where conflict already raged, though without the noise or confusion of human war. The spider's mouth is not adapted to the production of sound. Spiders have a method of thought transference which is distinct from telepathy, and dependent upon actual nerve contact. But noise is a vulgarity to which they do not descend. They will be silent, whether they kill or die.

Only a few minutes before, spiders had died without being seen by their companions, without appearing to arouse any excitement among them for long moments.

That was when Jalna, having been installed in the thickest part of a great tree (with Gleda at her side), too far from the ground to be reached from below, too low to be reached from above, and among branches too dense for the intrusion of anything much beyond human bulk, had grown tired of waiting. If she could kill some of these monsters before they were roused to violence themselves, was it not a clear gain?

She was some distance from the burning building, because the ground in front of it had already been cleared for about two hundred yards, and no spiders were working upon it. Beyond, there was about a similar length of ground where the spiders had removed all the major trees, and were occupied—about eighty of them in all—in rooting up the undergrowth. Still farther away, other spiders were dragging trees by silken ropes clear of the ground, the roots sometimes snapping, but more often coming up, as the teams dragged on the ropes.

Jalna, taking leisurely aim, and appearing as cool as when she shot at the butts (only she knew how her heart was beating then, conscious of critical eyes) had shot well.

Her first attempt was at a large female, who was engaged in tying up a bundle of uprooted bushes with a silk rope, so that it could be easily dragged away. It was an operation which had a human-seeming quality when being done on so large a scale, and yet of an elementary obviousness to a creature who could spin cocoons, traps, or dwellings.

As she moved round the bundle she roped, she turned her back to Jalna, so that the entrance to her spinnerets came into view, and Jalna, using her utmost strength, aimed at the left orifice of these, and knew that she had not missed, though she doubted whether those in ambush beneath her were aware of what she had done. For the arrow had entirely disappeared, and the spider, beyond a momentary restlessness of her hinder end, showed no consciousness of the attack.

"Well, that's that," Jalna said, philosophically. "I must try in another place."

"Isn't there a chance," Gleda suggested hopefully, "that it may have gone on to her heart? Anyway, I shouldn't think she'll spin much from that side in the future."

"I don't intend that she shall spin anything any more," Jalna answered, in a tone of vicious exasperation. "What about this?"

The spider was sideways now, and the shaft struck it in the narrow waist through which the main artery, the wind-pipe, and the great nerve centre must go, and for which there could be no space to spare. The arrow showed this time, buried for half its length in the spot at which Jalna had aimed. The spider moved one leg irritably in the air, and went on with its work.

"Why don't they *squeal*?" Jalna exclaimed, with added exasperation in her voice. "It isn't natural to go on like that." And then: "I wish I had Lemno's strength. I meant it to go right through."

"Well, you might try again."

"That's what I'm doing now."

This time nervous energy had its reward. The arrow, aimed at another spider now, passed out of sight, having penetrated completely through, and this time there was evidence of the damage which had been done. Green blood came in spurts from both sides.

Now the spider showed evident signs of discomfort, reaching back with first one leg and then another to a place which, from the position of its eyes, it could never see, and then gyrating rapidly, as though to catch up with the place where the trouble lay.

"That one," Jalna said, with a purr in her voice, "won't be any more trouble to us." She looked round for another victim.

The one she had shot first was moving back jerkily as though to push away an irritation it could not understand, but which would not cease. Doing this, she barged into a male of about half her size, who had his hands on a silken rope, and swung him round. The male spiders were never at ease with their cannibalistic mates. Even at such a time as this, instinctive terrors were hard to still. Now the spider, so incomprehensibly assaulted, did not wait for explanation to come. Dropping the rope, he leaped like a startled frog.

As he did so, the front of his body—a spider has nothing which would be proper to call a head—confronted Jalna. The creature was a long distance away, and was not at rest. The shot must be taken instantly, if at all. As it came down from its leap, the bow twanged. The arrow pierced the second lower eye from the right. It did not go in very far. Entering in a somewhat downward direction, it may have encountered bone.

The tormented, bewildered creature raised its right palp to the blinded eye. It may have meant to pull the shaft out. More probably, its intention was merely to find out what was wrong, or to push away whatever was causing that intolerable pain. What it did was to break the shaft. In blind, tormented fury, it rushed away.

It had been a marvellous shot!

Whether from that or other causes, it was evident from that moment that the spiders had become aware of danger, and were reacting in a bold way. They left their work, and came hurrying toward the place where the ambush hid.

It was at this moment that the smoke rose from behind the dome, followed almost instantly by a torrent of raging fire, and Relf gave the word that released a volley of arrows.

Lemno, emerging from behind the blaze, had a monstrous vision of waving palpi and high-jointed scurrying legs.

He saw one spider, close to the wood, being attacked by a group of out-running men, who thrust pokers into its belly, and hacked with axes and knives at the lowest joints of its sensitive, hairy legs. But it did not wince or withdraw. The spiders had no battle cries, nor did they give any sounds of pain or alarm. They moved on feet that made no sound unless something they encountered should be broken or thrust aside. There was little evidence of emotion or excitement in what they did, apart from the rapidity with which they moved.

But they were not moving to get away. They were fighting now.

CHAPTER XXX.

VICTORY!

LEMNO saw the spider rushing upon him. Its body was of the bulk of an elephant, but it had an appearance of far greater size, through the extent of its many legs, of which the top joints were far above the height of the rounded back.

He stood his ground, as he had given orders that all must do. An arrow leaped from his bow, hitting the aperture of the mouth fairly enough, between the crushers from which it would have rebounded vainly. It was a shot which Jalna could not have excelled, but whether it would have been sufficient to save his life he would never know, for at that moment another spider came rushing blindly out of the burning building. Its cephalothorax smoked; the spines of its legs had been scorched away. It had an odour of burning flesh. It collided with the one who would have made Lemno her meat, so that there was a confusion of waving legs. Whether the spider who sustained this unexpected assault acted with intelligence, or was confused and maddened by the pain of the arrow which had disappeared into her mouth, there was no hesitation in what she did. The claws of her palpi sank into the abdomen of her burnt companion, and next moment the poison fang was driven deeply into the soft skin.

Almost instantly the frantic struggles of her victim subsided into quieter motions, which became less and less, and would soon be none.

Lemno had dodged round to the farther side of this unexpected and unconscious rescue. Being a male, it was only about half the size of the one by which it had been destroyed, but there was shelter for the man who crouched under the quietening legs, for which he must endure the stench of the body, which was like that of a caldron of boiling fat.

With deliberate care he shot his remaining arrows.

112

The spider who had threatened him before had moved away, taking a zigzag course, as though less conscious of where she went than of her own distress, but there was no lack of others at which to shoot. The whole cleared space had become a pandemonium of almost noiseless conflict. The silence of the spiders was absolute, and if a spider should overcome one of her antagonists, she would be neat and instant in what she did.

Lemno remained under the shelter of the burnt carcass until the heat from the flaming building upon his back became too great to be endured any longer. Then he moved out, poker in hand, to join a scene of confused conflict, the issue of which was still very far from sure.

From wood to wood, across the extent of the open land, were spiders, squirming, twisting, seizing and killing, surrounded by dodging men who hacked at slender limbs, or thrust upward at soft bellies, while the snipers' arrows whizzed from the wood.

It was a fight which went on for a breathless, interminable time which no man measured, until, suddenly, it was won.

By whatever signal, or concerted decision, such spiders as still had uninjured brains to guide them, and sufficient legs to bear them away, with sudden unanimity fled the field.

And Lemno, his left arm hanging too bruised for use, but otherwise free from hurt, was left to congratulate his men, and to count the price of the victory they had won.

CHAPTER XXXI.

A MEAL AFTER VICTORY

THE cost of victory was found to be seventeen men killed, and four so maimed that they were destroyed immediately. There were three others who appealed to Lemno for his protection to let them live. There were many who had bruises and wounds—and no complaints. Potential additions to a restricted larder are indisposed to ask for nurses or beds without urgent cause.

Actually, it was this aspect of the success which had been won that was least satisfactory to those who had risked their lives for its achievement. Victory should mean that the fires will glow, and the joints roast when the night is near, and there is impatience among exhausted and hungry men. It should mean that, while able-bodied foes will have run away, the enemy dead and wounded will have been left; and if they are not good for roasting, what is?

But the spiders were not. There had been attempts to eat them in earlier times, but they had a flavour which rendered even their muscles intolerable to human palates. Those who eat spiders (such men there are) say that they should be swallowed whole, which it was clearly impossible to attempt.

There were ten of the huge females and three males. The fact that there were two-thirds of females among the dead may be most plausibly attributed to the fact that the male spider habitually lives the warier life. The female spider has two dominant passions: to feed and breed. She is singularly unswerving and ruthless in their pursuit. The male spider, being so much weaker than she, can gratify both these passions to her equal satisfaction, but he looks at matters more discriminately.

When to this different technique of living we add the fact that the male spiders were less than half the size of the females, and that while the female palpi terminated in very formidable claws, those of the male had hands only, and these primarily shaped for amatory caresses, it will be readily understood that the males had shown more wariness of approach to the scene of conflict, and (which had been the particular advantage) had been less frequently preferred as targets for the bowmen's shafts.

Useless for food these ten bodies certainly were, but Lemno considered them from another angle, and asked himself if he were content, and was less than sure. The quality of his victory must depend upon facts at which he could only guess—the number of their foes who were badly mauled, or would die of the wounds they had, and the effect of the defeat on the morale of those who fled.

There was also the substantial loss the enemy had sustained in the deaths of the moulting spiders. It seemed unlikely that such a building would have been duplicated, or that such an opportunity would occur again. He saw that he had won a victory: he could not be equally sure that he had won a campaign.

But there were more immediate matters with which to deal, and the first of these must be the appeal of the wounded men. The mere fact that it had been brought to him, instead of being decided by those into whose hands they first came, was a proof of the ascendancy he was obtaining, which he did not fail to observe.

The wounded men had friends—one of them had several—who were unwilling that they should die, and there was a little crowd of disputants who looked to Lemno to decide what should be done.

The spokesman of those who would put hunger and custom before possibility of saving their comrades' lives was a rather short, plump man, whose waistline suggested that he must have been more successful than had been most of the lean figures around him in finding food during recent weeks. He was emphatic that the injured men would not live, and that it was reason to finish them before they wasted away. "One of them," he said, "is so clawed that his lungs are bare."

Gleda and Jalna had come to Lemno a few minutes before. Jalna still wore the fur, and had her bow in her hand. She was in an exultant mood, having been praised by all, and by Lemno last. Gleda, beside her, had not even the fibre tunic which was common to all. She also was elated with victory, and somewhat reconciled to Jalna by the comradeship of danger and excitement which had been theirs in the trees. She heard the dispute, and she had a special sympathy with the wounded man, which is easy to understand. She said: "He must have been a brave man to be wounded thus. A man with a pierced lung may still live. I have known it to be."

Lemno looked at her in a way that showed he would have preferred it should have been left to him. But then he looked at the man, and said: "Now, Gobi, will you answer to that?"

The man turned his eyes on Gleda with some contempt. He saw the fur on Jalna's shoulders. He saw also that Gleda was unclothed, as she would not have been had not the stress of battle come almost with Jalna's return (but he could not know that), and he saw red weals and scratches from head to heel. It was clear to him where Lemno's favour was placed. Probably there was a suggestion which he would be glad to hear from another tongue. He said: "What is it to you that the man die? I should say that your mind should be on the end for which you were brought here. It is a time of feast when all should give of the best they have; and most of those who are dead are but husks which the spiders have sucked dry."

He turned his eyes to Lemno, as though asking that he should give to others that which he did not need.

Lemno said: "Gobi, there is a wound in your own belly. Have you seen that?"

Gobi looked down, as any man, hearing such words, would be certain to do. What he saw was the point of Lemno's poker as it went in.

Lemno looked round a surprised ring. He asked: "Are there others who would teach me what I should do?"

When he was met by silence, he added: "I will see the hurt men myself. For this night they shall live. There is meat here. How did he get so fat?"

The last question was adroit to withdraw sympathy from the man whose screams were subsiding now. Lemno was learning fast how to rule.

CHAPTER XXXII.

LEMNO USES PLAIN WORDS

LEMNO spoke to Jalna apart. He said: "You did well. You have great skill with the bow, and you have shown yourself to be one who does not fail when the need is most. I gave you public praise, which was due. Now I speak of more private things. You wear a coat which should have been given back many hours ago. I did not say this at a sooner hour, because I watched what you would do of your own will.

"Now I will tell you this: I choose my own wives, be they one or more. I am not to be told what I would have. You may do well for yourself if you think of that."

Jalna concealed her thoughts, as prudence urged her to do; but she saw that there was hope in the last words. She was pert in reply: "You are not to take, as I have some sense to see. And I will say that neither am I. I could have choice tonight of five hundred men—excepting those who are hurt or dead. But I lie alone of my own will."

She went to Gleda, to whom she returned the fur, with words which she did not think would be told to Lemno, which she would not have wished. She said: "I have done with this, for which I must give you thanks. It has been useful to me.

"But I must not let men mistake me for Lemno's wife. He is not one to wed. He is too quick at providing meat. It is as your friend that I say you should be very watchful of that."

Gleda showed no annoyance at this. She only replied: "But have you thought that Lemno's judgment is good?"

Jalna could make what she liked of that. Jalna did not attempt to make a third with them that night. She saw that it might mean a rebuff, which would have been hard to endure.

Lemno talked to Gleda, his mind having been stirred by the events which he had controlled, and which were controlling him. He was glad to speak his thoughts to one who had both wit to understand, and loyalty not to betray what was said, of both of which he was sure.

He was less sure that she would approve all he had done, and found that he was right in that doubt.

She said: "He was a man I had no reason to like, for he would have had no mercy on me. But he should not have been served as he was. It was not just. I may be wrong. But that was its appearance to me."

"And you suppose others may think so too?"

"How should I know that? They are your people, not mine. And they look to you, as to one who is born to lead. You may do much now, either for evil or good."

"Do I not see that? And did you think I would defend what I have done? It was unjust. It was an impulse I should have ruled. How can a man rule others who is misled by himself?

"But there was a saying which I have read in the records of other days. It was that power corrupts, and that if power be absolute, corruption will be absolute too. Am I one who will prove its truth? I must hope not.

"But it seems to me that this is the eternal problem which men have sought vainly to solve since they joined as nations or tribes, and it may be the rock on which they will always split, either soon or late. And if we cannot find those who will rule justly and well, what is left to hope? We must be spiders or ants.

"Either each must go his own way, as the spiders do, not even making a home, by way of being free of constraint; or they can go to the communist way that the ants prefer, having no freedom at all.

"Of these two, I would say that the way of the spiders is to be preferred, for I think that liberty can be bought at a high price, and yet not at more than its value is. But I observe this: when the spiders are at a great need, they combine; they submit themselves to a common plan, and there must be meaning in that.

"Union is added strength, and it can win much which can be gained in no other way. It is the method of choice as to who shall lead which is so hard to resolve. It is that which has led us to where we are—where none rules, but all must yield to the common will.

"Yet, as the scene will change (which is never still), can we maintain that? We have crossed but a river's width, and I may be king, if I will, of five hundred men—that is, if the spiders should be defeated, which we may hope but not know."

Gleda said: "There are many doubts, but one thing that is sure. We should sleep now."

118

"I have learned before now," he laughed, "that you counsel well."

CHAPTER XXXIII.

A SIGNAL OF DISTRESS

"LORD," a man said in a humble voice, "you will forgive that I break your rest. There is a messenger here with most urgent news."

Lemno waked at once. He rose in such a way that Gleda, who had not stirred, was still covered. He noticed, with some satisfaction, the term of address which the man had used, but his thought went on to wonder what messenger there could be, or what urgent news, while all his men were around him there.

Were the spiders about his rear? Had he been too quick to assume that the fight was done? After all, nine spiders (not counting the ones which had been burned) were not many.

"Messenger?" he asked. "From whom? Bring him to me."

"He comes from the farther bank. He will speak to you."

"Well, so he can."

The man who came was a stranger to him. He was not clean, and he had a bandage round his left leg.

"I come from Mendrale," he said. "He seeks you, and at great need."

"Does he think I have men to spare? I have needs here."

"But ours is instant and great."

"Would it turn the scale? And how many would be needed for that? Does he ask that I cast him the winning die?"

"He has no thought to win. It is to get clear."

"And after that? But you shall tell me the tale, and we will talk of that which is clearly shown. And may I know what office and name is yours?"

"I am Coxo. I came myself, being second only to him."

"Then you are he who was most urgent to spoil my plan."

"Yes. I am he. I will not say I was wrong. Five hundred men on the first day—"

"Would have been harder to feed. Yet you may say that. And I may say that we should have had little toil had we been all here. Let it be. Let us have the tale."

Lemno saw that a man of Coxo's importance would not have come at less than a vital need. He said: "Wait a moment. There is one who should hear what you will say."

He roused Gleda who sat up in a yawning mood.

Coxo looked surprised. "Is it not she…?"

"So it is. That is why she should hear. Gleda, here is tale of that which has been in your own land, of which you may understand more than I should be equal to do."

Gleda was awake now. "Is it well?"

"Is it well for whom? Let us listen first, and then talk."

Coxo said: "I will tell in the fewest words. We are driven back to the river bank. About five hundred men, being half of those who are left, are there, and are not yet molested at all. But about the same number are cut off, and compassed on every side. It seems that we may escape, if we leave them, which Mendrale is not willing to do. Neither am I."

"By what you say I may conclude that the same number as those they trap are either wounded or dead?"

"So you may. On either side the pots steam. But our loss has been greater than theirs, as may be forecast when those who invade are met with stout hearts, and with ambush and barricade. But we think that, if you should come at once, with every man that you have, and we should attack during the next night, which they would not expect us to do, we might get them free."

"So you might. It is what you should judge better than I. But there is one thing that might yet be fatal to us. Have you thought how we should get back?"

Coxo blinked at that. For he had seen it to be the greatest danger that there could be, and he did not welcome its intrusion so quickly to Lemno's mind. It confirmed what he had thought before, that in the end Lemno might be the greatest obstacle to his gaining the place for which he thought himself to be fit, and which Mendrale was not likely to keep.

It was from that fear that he had opposed Lemno's plan at the first, and it had been he who had originated the idea that they should go separate ways. He had not thought that Mendrale would hold the ascendancy which he had gained, and that doubt had been confirmed by the events of the last days; but now that they had become nearly fatal for all, he must appear the one to avert greater danger. That was why he was here.

He said: "Some could swim."

"And most not. There might be more lost that way."

Coxo avoided that to which it would have been hard to make convincing reply. He said: "There is no time to be spared. If you would move at once to the bank, we would have the canoes on this side, so that men could cross during the night. You have done well here?"

"We have begun in the right way. I will not say more than that. Have you fed?"

"I was in too much haste. I have come on through the night."

"Then you shall now. You shall have a portion of Gobi's loins, which has been kept for our morning meal."

"Gobi was killed?"

"He died of greed. We can let him be. When the meal is done, I will tell you how I decide."

Coxo did not like the sound of that, but must be content for the time. He did not think it wise to show anxiety as to what Lemno might do or refuse. But Lemno was in a difficult doubt.

Gleda watched him with a mental sympathy which saw his problem much in the same way, though it had another angle for her. She felt refreshed by her long sleep, and content that Jalna had been much farther away than on the previous night. She felt some stiffness when first she moved, and her left side must be watched with care, but otherwise she was well at ease, both in body and mind.

She enjoyed her breakfast, reflecting that those who said that the flesh of men had a good taste were not wrong, and that she was fated to eat the flesh of those who had talked about eating her, which gave a sense both of justice and pleasure to what she did. She was silent until the meal was done, leaving Lemno to his own thoughts, which Coxo also was too cautious to interrupt. But then she said: "Could we speak apart?"

Lemno looked at both her and Coxo with expressionless eyes He may have judged that Coxo did not like the suggestion, which was natural enough, considering that Gleda was of their foes, but it was not a matter which would endure intrusion from him.

Lemno said: "As you will," and would have risen, but Coxo saw that courtesy would be costless, or might even bring a profit to him. He said: "But I can retire," and withdrew a short distance under the trees.

Lemno said: "This is of your country; or of that which was yours. What would you have?"

"Suppose that I could make peace for all?"

"It would be much to hope. How would you do that?"

"I might find reasons for letting the trapped men free, if we should thereafter avoid the land."

"How could they know that such a pledge would be kept?"

"They would take my word."

"You believe that?"

"Have you known me to lie?"

"No. I will allow that."

"Have you never thought that I may have honour in my own land? Have you ever asked who I am?"

"I asked your name on the first day."

"Which I told. It meant nothing to you?

"I will only say this: I do not offer to go if you can think of a better way. But I tell you this also. I do not think you will get those men free, and across the river in the few canoes which you have, without so much loss as will be a disaster to you. And if you lose, you lose all. You may be back with your books, as you say you wish, or you may be dead, but all this will be gone.

"If they chase you down to the river's brink, as I think they will, whether you have freed those who are trapped, or been repulsed in that also, they will not stop there. Why should they? You have shown them that this land can be taken with bows. They are very good with the bow."

"You think highly of what they can do."

"We agreed that we would talk sense. You should ask Coxo for an opinion on that. I did not think that they would be conquered by two thousand men, and those who went became fewer, as though numbers were of no moment at all."

"You would go alone? How should I know you would come back?"

"Do you ask me that? You are the one who should know."

"You might find you were less than free."

"If I should stay there, would you lose much?"

"I should lose you, which I should prefer to avoid."

She smiled: "You may let me go with a quiet mind."

"I could not do that. How can I know that they would let you return?"

"You must trust me when I say that that is not the danger to fear. There are those who will not wish me to stay."

"You could be plainer than that."

"So I could, if this were the time for a long tale. We should be moving while we talk."

"You think it to be so urgent as to require that?"

"I am sure. Coxo was right on that point. Your men may not be alive now. If you call him, you can tell him we are agreed. You can see how he frets!"

So they could. The length of the talk had led Coxo to conclude that they were plotting something together. He was pacing impatiently up and down, and casting glances in their direction which they were not meant to ignore.

Lemno smiled at her as he asked: "Did you say 'agreed'?"

"So I did. But there is one point which can be improved. You are right—perhaps I can do nothing alone. You must come with me."

He gasped. "Do you think me a fool?"

"Not at all. I think you are wise and also brave, as few wise men are. I tell you that we can succeed together, but that I can do nothing alone. If you do not agree, we shall be as good friends as before; but you will understand that there is nothing that I can do."

Lemno thought quickly, which was not a habit with him. He saw that her refusal to go alone showed that she was not simply aiming at escape to her own people. But might not this be a design to make her revenge upon him complete, putting him in the place he had once meant for her?

But he did not believe this; and he decided that it must be risked. He saw no clear way by which disaster could be avoided both on the right hand and on the left, if he should refuse this offer from her.

It was actually Gleda who decided for him when she said: "It is well that you have Relf, whom you can trust."

"You mean we should leave him in charge while we are away?"

"Yes. He is a true friend; and will be discreet in control. I am glad that you said 'we'. You will find that in trust there is double strength."

Lemno did not answer that. He called Coxo, to whom he said: "You can return at your best pace, and say that I follow at a near hour. If it is not too late, I will save those who are trapped. You will need to hurry, or I shall pass you on the way."

These were words which Coxo had been asking to hear, but they were said in a way which he did not like. It was too nearly the way in which a servant would be instructed to go, and there was no explanation of the long discussion with Gleda. But Lemno saw the discontent on his face. He saw also that there would be no gain in antagonizing a man whom he disliked, but with whom he might have to deal in the coming days, and he added quickly: "You can also say that I will not finally decide what is best until we have talked together—Mendrale and you and myself."

"Well," Coxo said, "it is time that is of most importance. I can see that it may take you an hour, or perhaps two, to make dispositions here and array your men. I will return at once and give Mendrale the word."

Lemno said nothing to that. Let them think he was bringing his troop if they would. It saved words. With satisfaction, he watched Coxo depart.

CHAPTER XXXIV.

IN HER OWN LAND

GLEDA sat in an upstairs room, having come again to a house in her own land. She looked out on a prospect of pleasant trees just turning to autumn gold. The scene was as rural as that which she had known for the short time that she had been the mistress of Lemno's house, and the trees were the same, but the house itself was larger and was of two floors. She had been in it before, when its land had not been trampled as it now was. But she had found no one in it whom she knew. They were slain or fled.

It was the best house which had been built in these parts, which was why Mendrale had taken it for his own quarters, for he was one who thought that a leader's dignity should be sustained. There are some who cannot rule without assertion of rank, and others who can.

Now Lemno conferred with Mendrale and Coxo, while Gleda, being unknown to those who passed in and out, had been put in this upper room for safety.

She had told Lemno much of how affairs had been in her own land before he snatched her away, and of the way in which she thought she might help free the encircled men without further shedding of blood. He had agreed: the plan was good.

"But," she had added, "I should say that it would be well to keep this from others, unless they are discreet."

"Mendrale," he had replied, "has no discretion at all. He will learn little from me."

Well, he might be hearing little, but, if so, it seemed that he or Coxo must be talking for a long time, for the conference had started an hour before. Gleda felt it to be a waste of time which must be endured. She looked idly out on beds which had been bright with flowers, but were now trampled beneath many indifferent feet.

She saw two men of her own race being hauled with ropes which would have tightened around their necks had they slackened pace. They were wearied and streaked with blood, and one limped, so that it was hard for him to make the pace that he must.

The men who brought them were hailed by the sentries who kept the door. "Take them," they said, "round to the long shed at the back. The butcher has been waiting for them there for the last hour."

Gleda did not stop to think. The men must be saved. She ran down.

She caught up with the procession of death as it rounded the side of the house. She said: "Those men are not to be killed. There will be new orders for you to hear."

There were four men dragging the two. They had not been neighbours of where Lemno had dwelt. She did not know them, nor they her.

They answered with respect, seeing the torn fur which she wore. But respect was the most it claimed. It did not require that they should take orders from her.

They said: "We know nothing of that. We deliver and our part is done. It is to the cook you should talk."

One of the others whispered: "Who is she? Her speech not ours."

The first man, though still without rudeness, asked: "Mistress, may I ask who it is who would give orders to us?"

"I am Lemno's wife. We have come to save those who are trapped.

Comprehension came to his eyes. "Then these men are of your folk. It is bad for you to see. But Mendrale will need his meal. You can talk to the cook."

Gleda saw that this proposal was not gravely meant. He had put her aside. They were stirring their charges to movement again.

She said quickly: "There is more in this than you think. They are to be exchanged for those of ours who are caught."

There was a moment's pause at this, but no more. They said: "Be that as it may, it is not to us you should speak," and at that moment the butcher came from the shed.

There was a scowl on his face as he said: "You were late before. Come on—bring the beasts in."

Gleda saw the knife in his hand. She said: "But they are not to be killed." All that had been said before must be said again to this one, and he had no patience. He said: "Mistress, you waste time which I cannot spare. I have no such orders."

She replied: "I will speak to Mendrale now. You shall have the order without delay."

He answered: "I will wait three minutes, and may be blamed for as much as that. I am late now."

She went back into the house. The sentries, who had seen her run out, let her return with no obstruction from them; but there was one at the door of the conference who was of a different mind.

He was a big stolid man, without symbol of authority except the knife in his hand, for there were no uniforms or badges of any kind among these volunteers, but it was naked and long and very persuasive.

He said: "I do not warn twice. If you attempt to pass me again, you must expect to see your own blood. No one must pass here until the door opens from inside."

"But I tell you it will not wait. Will you go yourself, and ask Lemno to come?"

He shook his head. "You'll wait for them to come out."

Gleda thought: "I might wait an hour," for she heard a murmur of voices within which went on like a brook. And then Lemno's voice rose, so that his words could be heard through the door. "Then there is no more to be said. It is in your own fat you must fry."

But she did not care what the words might be. If she could hear him he would hear her. She called loudly: "Lemno! Lemno!"

The sentry said: "Must you have a slit throat, or will you be still without that?"

His knife threatened her as he spoke, but at the same instant Lemno threw open the door. He was an angry man.

CHAPTER XXXV.

AN INTERRUPTED CONFERENCE

COXO had returned at a good pace, and though those who followed had not been far behind, they had not caught up with him. The way by the river bank had become a well-trampled path, and what had taken a day and more to do was now a matter of no more than a few hours. Lemno and Gleda got into a waiting canoe, and having but two miles of a good road on the farther side, they were at Mendrale's door while the sun was still high.

Mendrale did not appear to have been in any bustle of war, as Coxo certainly had. When he met Lemno, at what had become his own gate, with an outstretched hand, he was unwounded, and his garments were neat and clean. But neither did he appear to have slept well. His eyes were red, and his lips blue.

He said: "I see you have come with speed. How soon will they be here? Will they be ready to cross at dusk? I would be glad to know that."

Lemno avoided direct reply. He asked: "Can we talk in a quiet room?"

Mendrale replied: "So we can. You will not say you refuse aid?"

"Should I come so far to say that? But if you will say where my wife can wait, so that she will not be disturbed—"

Mendrale looked at Gleda without curiosity or apparent recognition. He said: "There is a room above into which none will go without my leave." He gave instructions, and she went upstairs and out of his harassed mind.

He told the sentry at the door of his own room that they were not to be disturbed, and led Lemno to a table at which Coxo already sat. There was nothing else alive there except a parrot, which had been unable to flee with the others.

Lemno said: "Tell me first how matters now stand."

Mendrale, whose life had demonstrated that, though words are less exhausting than deeds, they may be as potent for those who handle them with sufficient skill, described the landing and the advance which had been made, showing a tendency to defend or exalt himself.

Lemno was conscious that some things might have been put differently.

The landing had been unobstructed, and for the first two days they had met with no opposition whatever. The first day they had plundered houses from which the occupants had fled in such haste that they had left their contents almost intact. Their larders had been full and there had been plenty of pigs to slaughter. For it was evident that, though crops might have suffered from drought, the herds had not been diseased.

Even the effects of the drought must have been much reduced by a system of irrigation which had cut many narrow channels of water through the land. Also, the movements of the swine had been controlled by long fences, which penetrated the woods, and equalized their distribution. Fenced gardens were round the houses, which were otherwise very similar to those they had left behind, and scattered among the trees in the same way.

The second day had been like the first, except that the houses were barer, and the pigs had been driven away, but the absence of opposition created a problem of strategy, on which Coxo had been overruled.

On the first day, plunder had hindered advance. The second had seen less to take, and men had spread farther out. It was evident that this was rendering them more vulnerable to attack. The forest land was flat and featureless. There was the river behind them, offering a very poor means of retreat, for they had few canoes, while to right, to left, or ahead, it seemed that they could go as far as they would, and take as much as they could eat, or could bear away.

They had come expecting to fight, and hoping that they could win. They were confused and puzzled by the absence of any visible foe.

Then Mendrale had said: "It is clear that they had no heart to fight, seeing so many of us so well armed. But what use is their flight to us, if they strip the land? We must group and advance faster, and give them no time to move their herds and larders."

But Coxo had been more cautious. "Every mile that we spread out must be a help to them. I do not believe that they have fled in panic. What they have done has been the best strategy for them, and

130

the worst for us. If we spread ourselves any farther, we are asking to fill their pots with our own bones."

"Then," Mendrale had asked, "What would you do?" Which was hard to answer.

In the end, it was agreed that they should draw their men together for the third day, with outposts set to give warning of any hostile approach, sending out scouts to discover how far the land had been vacated, and if there were signs of any enemy force being gathered.

But of four scouts, three did not return, and the fourth, who may have used discretion more than his legs, reported that he had found nothing but a deserted hamlet, the site of a hand-weaving industry, a few miles ahead. He professed to have gone much farther without finding signs of life, which we may believe if we will.

The existence of the hamlet was confirmed by a large scale map, covering an area of not more than fifteen miles to southward, which had been found in one of the houses, and Mendrale decided that it should be occupied and plundered the following day.

It was agreed that Coxo, with seven hundred men, should advance to the occupation of the abandoned hamlet, while Mendrale would hold a similar number in reserve, with their base still on the river bank, and a thin line of pickets occupying the intervening road.

The way in which the herds of swine had been controlled had required that the major roads should be fenced against them, and these fences, of close-set wooden boards, were a complete screen, to a height of about four feet, on both sides of the roads. These roads were more clearly defined, and much better kept, than those to which Coxo had been accustomed, and the expedition, marching in good order in ranks of four, made rapid progress, which may not have been lessened by a light rain, which fell during the morning and then ceased.

They surrounded the hamlet, and then sent scouts into it, who found it vacant, as had been reported before. The caution of their approach had done them no good, but it gave them a feeling of confidence. Coxo, they felt, was one who would take no risks.

It was evident that much had been removed, especially food, but there are always things which such an exodus overlooks, and they had soon collected as much spoil as they could carry away. And the items which had been overlooked included one piece of real luck. The hamlet had not confined its activities to the weaving of cloth. It had included a bacon factory, the main storeroom of which had been cleared to the last knuckle, but there was a smaller one which had been entirely overlooked—probably because someone delegated for the clearance had been unfamiliar with the building—and from the roof of this room had hung forty succulent hams.

Coxo had considered those hams. He had considered them both in themselves and their implications. He considered them worth more than the fresh and complete carcasses of the twenty or more pigs from which they had come. He had hurried back to Mendrale with a proposal which he thought, not without logical probability, would both increase their own prestige and relieve them from further anxiety as to their position.

This was to send back the canoes, loaded with food, including those priceless hams, and invite not only Lemno's five hundred, but larger numbers from their own country, to join them in exploiting so rich a land.

For did not those hams disclose that the people here were not merely well-fed? They had food to spare! They cured bacon and hams, as those who feel hunger are never likely to do. The sight of those hind legs should bring reinforcements in such numbers that they could advance on a much broader front, and with guarded flanks.

Coxo's idea was sound, but it came too late. He had actually been in conference with Mendrale, with a ham conspicuously placed on the table before them, when the news bad come that the expeditionary force was being attacked upon every side.

Faced by this crisis, Coxo appeared to have acted with energy and courage. "I got together..."—he said, taking the tale out of Mendrale's mouth, and turning to Lemno, who had been a silent listener to this point—"I got together every man that I could at a quick call—about four hundred, I should say, but we didn't waste time to count—and set off down the south road. I sent scouts right and left, in four parties of three each, to make sure that we shouldn't fall into any trap. I thought that those fences were going to be the devil for us, and that's just what they were.

"One of the twelve came back, with an arrow sticking out of his shoulder, and but for that I don't suppose I should be here now. He said the other two with him had been killed with arrows, and he had escaped, as he did, because he had stopped to get a thorn out of his foot. That was just before they came to a cross-fence, and, when the other two got close before he did, the bowmen ambushed there had to let fly. It's a safe guess that the other nine got killed in about the same way.

"Well, we knew what to expect then; but that didn't tell us how to deal with it.

"Two hundred yards ahead, if we left the road, we should find wood fences before us on both sides—solid fences, four feet high to divide the pigs, and with arrows coming through slits which had been cut in them, as well as over the top.

"If we didn't like that, we could go on, four or five abreast, along a road which was fenced both sides, and ambushed with bowmen as thick as lice.

"We'd got too much sense, or too little stomach, for that. I made a show of attacking to hold them to where they were, and sent word back for the men behind to all scramble over the left-hand fence when a whistle blew, and run hard through the trees, to try to scale the cross-fence farther away, before the other side would be likely to have many men there. It was the right thing to do, and it put us more or less on equal terms, but it couldn't do more than that. And it didn't alter the fact that they were about three to one, and better disciplined and better armed than our men."

Lemno asked: "How?"

"They've got more bows; and instead of pokers they've got a kind of long-handled bill-hook that gives horrible wounds, and they handle them as though they've been drilled."

"What do you mean when you say they are better disciplined?"

"They wear coloured stripes on their arms, and those with stripes of the same colour make a unit that acts together according to how their whistles blow."

"Well, go on."

"It's a short tale from there. We fought them until about all those who were willing to be killed were dead, and then we ran back with them hanging on, and sending arrows after us most of the way.

"After that, we made two further attacks—one from a different direction, and one during the night—by which we lost a lot of men, and killed some of theirs, but did no good for ourselves. Our men are still shut up, and, apart from the fact that the attacks on them never cease, and they are getting fewer and weaker all the time, we know that their water is nearly done, and, unless it should rain, they can't hold out beyond tomorrow. They must yield on whatever terms they can get, or die of hunger and thirst, which is a poor choice for them to have."

Coxo finished his tale, and Mendrale added: "You will understand, now you have heard, why I have been so anxious, and still am, to have a clear assurance from you that your men will be here by tomorrow's dawn. Can you not say the one word which will end the doubt?"

"I have said," Lemno replied, "that I should not have come so far to refuse aid."

"Then they will be here?"

"You do not ask whether I cannot help you in other ways."

"Because there is no other that can get them free in the time we have."

"You may be wrong in that. I have brought one who may help in another way."

Mendrale stared at this without comprehension, but Lemno saw a measure of understanding in Coxo's eyes—and little hope of support.

His glance said: "So we are about to hear what I saw you plot." But when he spoke it was smoothly enough.

"If you will tell us how you will get them free, we shall be most grateful."

"You know that I took my wife from this land?"

"All men know that."

"Have you thought that she might give good counsel, where force has failed?"

"Why should she do that? Would she not prefer her own kin, even though she may have become yours in a rough way? I should say you did rashly to bring her here. But I would not intrude on that which is your matter rather than mine."

Mendrale had listened to these exchanges with scowling eyes. Now he said: "I had not thought who she is! Does she know our plans? It was reckless to bring her here."

Lemno was unmoved. He said: "She cannot know plans which are not agreed. But she has one of her own, which you should hear."

Mendrale held to his point: "Does she know what we have asked of you?"

Coxo's voice interposed: "Yes. She knows that. There were no secrets from her."

Mendrale rose. "I will give orders that she shall not escape. She could betray all."

Lemno was between him and the door. He said: "She will betray nothing. But you will listen to me, or I will go back in the next hour, and your men will be soon dead, and yourself shamed."

Coxo said: "What is done is done. Let us hear what he would say now."

The tone held a sneer which made the words worse than they need have been, but perhaps this was helpful in bringing Mendrale back to his seat. If he were taking advice, it was from one who was clearly not upon Lemno's side.

Lemno said: "You knew she came from this land, but you do not know who she is."

"No," Coxo replied. "Do you say you do? And what may that be to us?"

"She is the elder sister of the man who we may conclude to be ruling now."

Mendrale asked: "What of that? Will he loose hostile men from his net at a sister's plea?"

Coxo asked, with more venom behind his words: "Will you say how long you have known that?"

"I was told that this dawn, while you were standing aside."

"Then, if it may be said in a friendly way, I should call it a very evident lie. The folk here are not as simple as we. They dress so that their ranks are shown. Had she been attired as a queen when you roped her in, you would have guessed much, and have asked her more."

"You have not considered that she may not have been clothed at all? Listen: I landed the canoe far down the bank, at the very head of the falls. Then I took it upstream, and I hid it, where bushes spread.

"It was there that I saw a woman dive. I suppose that her clothes were there, but they were nothing to me. I watched while she swam, during which time the current carried her down, as you know it would. Then she landed, doubtless intending to walk up to her clothes, as it may have been habit to do, believing herself to be alone. I roped her. She had the wit to be silent, or she would not be alive now."

"She may have wit," Mendrale said, "Yet she may not fool all of us. Can we not talk of a better plan?"

But Coxo was shrewd enough to see that there might be more in this than he had first thought. He asked: "Has she a plausible plan? And why should she do so much for us, which you had not sought?"

"It is fairly asked," Lemno replied, "and when I tell you, you will see that we have a fair hope.

"When I caught her, an uncle who ruled all had just died, and she was his heiress. But if she were gone, then a brother would take her place. Do you suppose he will want her back now?"

Coxo's attention had become keen. He asked: "Is there help in that?"

"She can bargain that she will not return, if these men are freed."

"Will she do so much?"

"She is more content with the new life which we shall make in the land which we are expecting to gain."

Mendrale listened to this with a puzzled frown He did not like positions to be thrust upon him which were obscure in themselves, and on which he must make momentous decisions without delay. He was doing no more than thinking aloud, when he said, "She is to go alone, knowing all our plans, and how weak we are, to her own people, where she can be queen if she will, with much praise for the way in which she escaped and befooled us And they will destroy us knowing that we despair, and that there is no relief coming from you. Or again, she may mean well, and they may put her aside, which would be no better for us."

CHAPTER XXXVI.

MENDRALE SCHEMES ILL

AS Mendrale spoke, it was evident that the facts, as he put them, made it no better than a wild gamble to let Gleda go. As he finished, he looked to Coxo for support, which he thought he was sure to have. But Lemno spoke first.

"It is all much as you say, except that I know her as you do not. And you were wrong on one point. She would not go alone. She requires that I shall go too."

Coxo looked the amazement he felt. "You would do that? Did she spring it first, or did you?"

"She said that she might not succeed alone, for she might not be able to give a sufficient pledge."

Mendrale saw a joke. He said: "She would go with a full net. She has recalled that there are pots in her own land."

He looked at Lemno, his good humour restored by the jest. His expression said: is she so great a fool as to think you would do that?

Coxo took it differently. He judged that Lemno intended to go, and he did not think he would be easy to dupe. After all, this might be the one way—

He said: "It is clear to me, except that I do not see why they should doubt her pledge. Or, if they should, that yours would be much better for them to have."

"But that should surely be plain. Has she the right to pledge that we would not return with tenfold force on the next day, even though she should keep her own word and remain behind?"

This reply was followed by a short silence. It was evident that it disconcerted both of those who had heard.

Coxo was the first to speak. He said: "No. She could not pledge that. Neither could you."

"She says it would be needful to secure the freedom of those who are netted now. It would, of course, be on our pledge to her."

Mendrale and Coxo exchanged glances which agreed that it would not do. It would be utter defeat for them, though in another form from that which they had feared during recent hours.

Lemno saw, and partly understood, the blankness of their response. He added: "It is possible that it might also be arranged for a donation of food to be freely given, so that a spirit of goodwill should overlay what has occurred, and, beyond that, there might be lasting exchange. Have you thought that, if the spiders shall be destroyed, and their land free, there may be communication across it, such as will end the division the lower river has made?"

They considered this with the attention which it deserved. What its effects on their own fortunes might be was not instantly seen, but their minds, by different roads, soon came to the same point. It would be worthless to them—certainly so, unless they could take Lemno's place in the spiders' land. And the whole scheme did not suggest that there would be likelihood of that. It was Lemno who would have any praise there might be—he and his new wife.

Coxo's thought went further: a trade between the two countries would, of necessity, be carried on through Lemno's territory, and on which he could levy what toll he would.

It was bad enough to have had to appeal to Lemno for aid, but if that had enabled them to relieve their imperilled men, and then to retire to his territory with a larger force than he would control— well, there were possibilities, if not certainties, there for men of ingenious and perhaps unscrupulous minds. And in any case, there would be expectation that the tale of plenty which they would take back, with the ocular demonstration of those superfluous hams, would gather volunteers for an expedition which would be of sufficient strength to bring matters to a very different issue from that which annoyed them now.

But to retire disgraced and saved by Lemno's intervention, on a condition that they would never return—it would be hard indeed to get any praise for so poor a tale!

Realizing this, the same thought came to both, but it was Mendrale who gave it voice. He said: "Well, you can give the pledge. It will be no fault in you if it should prove to be one which you will be powerless to keep."

The words were followed by an ominous silence. Coxo, seeing the anger in Lemno's eyes, thought what a fool Mendrale had been to speak that which should have been silently thought, or whispered softly between themselves.

Lemno, controlling anger and fierce contempt, broke the pause of antagonistic silence by saying: "I don't agree with you that a pledge which I might give on behalf of our nation would not be honoured by us, after its condition had been irrevocably observed. But, however that may be, I should make no bargain with such a possibility in the rear of my own mind, though I might be content to leave it to be proved by the event. But one thing is certain, after what you have said, I will neither go myself, nor would I allow Gleda, if she were willing, to do so, unless I have your written promise to observe whatever terms I may make with them."

It was Mendrale's turn now to delay reply. He had the look of a cornered man. But, however much he might fear the alternative, it was a humiliation that he could not accept. He said: "You can't expect me to do that. But it's your pledge that's wanted, not mine. Anyway, that's what you told me the woman said, and you can take it I shan't interfere."

It was at this point that Lemno's patience had given way, and that he had told Mendrale that he could fry in his own fat (whatever that may have meant) in so loud a voice that it had been heard on the other side of the door.

CHAPTER XXXVII.

LEMNO BUYS TWO LIVES

"LEMNO," Gleda said, as he appeared at the door, "they are killing two of our men! It must be stopped!"

"They may kill whom they will. We are going back."

Neither of these hurried exchanges was very clear in meaning. Mendrale, following Lemno to the door, did not like the "our," which seemed to identify Gleda, if not Lemno, with their enemies, and Lemno's "they" might be meant for either side.

Mendrale burst out with: "What do you ask? It is I who give orders here."

"There are two men in the yard that they want to kill. It would spoil everything."

Coxo, who had kept his wits, said: "I will stop that for a time." He hurried into the yard.

Gleda followed him. The yard was bare, and the shed shut. She said: "You may be too late. They are in there."

"I know," he said curtly. He would have short speech with Gleda. This was not being done for her.

He entered the shed with Gleda closely behind him. One of the men was tied up, and the butcher reached for the knife.

As the door opened, the man's voice could be heard in frantic protest: "I tell you it was Her Highness herself. She will have you slaughtered for this!"

The butcher said: "You may spare your breath. I will wait no more," and would have plunged in the knife had he not heard the sound of the opening door, and Coxo's urgent voice: "Kimba, stop. They are not for tonight."

Kimba turned with a fearless scowl, which showed how little discipline there was in these ranks: "Then you should have told me before now. What are orders for, if they should not be obeyed?"

140

He looked from Coxo to Mendrale, who was now close behind him, his head showing over that of his shorter colleague, as though inviting a different decision.

Lemno's aloofness of mood, inclined to abstract reflection at any crisis, wondered whether such indiscipline might not be inevitable in the absence of penalizing law, and then recalled that his own men were of different conduct; the problem lay in the choosing of human leaders, from which his mind was diverted next moment by Mendrale's reply.

"That is for our friend, Lemno, to say. The question is, will he need them as guides, or not?"

Gleda heard this verdict with too confident a belief that she had won. It seemed a plausible reason for granting their lives, and would sound much better than if it had been made a favour to her.

But Lemno was slow to speak, and when he did, it was in the toneless way that gave no clue to his thoughts. All he said was: "You will let them live."

Mendrale said: "That is not enough. You must say why."

Lemno looked at him in a way that caused Gleda to think that, had his poker been in his hand, Mendrale might have learned how it felt, as another had done before. But he said: "They must live, for they come with me."

That was less than Mendrale had required, as they both knew, but his eyes sank, and he said no more.

The butcher was cutting them loose now, and Lemno looked at them with more care than before. He turned to another man, whom he had seen at the kitchen door, and who was now peering over Coxo's head: "You are the cook? So I supposed. You will give these men a good meal, and then they must come to me. I shall be in the front upper room on the left, where I shall be waiting for them. Come with me, Gleda. I have something to tell you."

Ignoring the other leaders, he led the way to the room where she had waited before.

He locked the door, turned to her. "I have saved them because you asked, and because it would have been madness to kill them. But I do not say that their lives are safe beyond the next hour. Neither are ours."

He told her what the conversation had been. "And now," he said, "you decide. Shall we go on? Is it good enough? And do I tell all to the brother from whom you buy? Or shall I leave it to you?"

Gleda replied at once, as though she had been asked no more than a little thing: "I shall trust you and be content. They are only scum. I do not think they could prevail against you and Relf, and those of the better sort. And it must be our secret for now. I can judge this better than my brother. We shall know more when Coxo comes."

"You have spoken a good word. You will not regret it. You think Coxo will come?"

"Yes. I am sure. I do not know what he will say, but it will be lies."

A few minutes later Coxo knocked at the door. He came in with a smile.

"You will have noticed," he began, "that I said nothing in Mendrale's support. It was awkward to have agreed to be second to him. But he is a fool, as I need not trouble to say. He will be no more trouble to you."

"I can see," Lemno said, "that you are a wiser man," which was a discreet reply, saying little and leaving much unsaid. He added: "I will do what I can; and quickly, if you will send the two prisoners to me. They have been fed by now."

CHAPTER XXXVIII.

THE PRICE OF PEACE

"THEY will not sit, I should guess, while you stand," Lemno said, "and their need will be much greater than mine." So when the two were brought in, there being but three chairs in the room, they were given two, and Lemno walked to the window, where he gazed down on many movements below.

"Highness," said the man with the damaged leg, "we owe you our lives; and I would beg you to know that we have not been faithless to you. We had all thought you drowned."

"I do not blame them. And I suppose my brother reigns, as he should?"

"Yes, Highness."

"Is he near?"

The man hesitated. He looked toward Lemno who might be supposed to be listening to what was said, though his back was to them. Distress was evident in the man's eyes.

"There is nothing," Gleda said, "which you may not tell. We shall make peace."

The man did not answer. He looked at his companion, who shook his head slightly.

The man said, miserably: "Highness, our lives are yours—"

Gleda smiled. "Very well, I will ask in a different way. Could you lead me to him?"

Even that question did not seem to be one which could be answered with ease. The man paused, choosing his words. "He could be found."

Lemno looked round. "There will be no need. I should say he is coming to us."

Gleda joined him at the window. The two, rising more stiffly, for they were spent men, followed. The road to the north was straight ahead. It was visible for a long way, and they saw the men who fled toward them, arrows flickering in their rear.

"Your brother," Lemno said, "seems to be a good man of war."

"It must be stopped," Gleda said. "We must act quickly."

Lemno spoke to the man whom Gleda had questioned before: "You would not say where the king is, because you knew he would be making an attack on this side, where we did not expect it?"

"Lord, could I betray that?"

"No. I can see that you are a loyal man. But you must understand. I am not against you at all. Will you take your will?"

"If I see the king," Gleda added, "all will be well, even now."

"Highness," said the man who had not spoken before, "it shall be as you will. What can we do?"

"I will tell you that—" Lemno began, and stopped to listen to a noise from the outside of the door. He walked to it, drew up the bolt, and called: "You can come in now!" But there was no response. He pulled the handle, but the door held. He said: "It has been made fast on the outside. What do you make of that?"

Gleda said: "They must be mad!"

"It is not our help they dislike. It is the way we play the game."

"Shall we break loose? I suppose we could."

"We will wait awhile; and tell our friends the situation."

For the moment, at least, his words had a prudent sound. It was surely safer here than in the bicker without, where it might be hard to tell who were friends or foes.

They might have been more troubled had they heard the plan that Coxo had whispered in Mendrale's ear a few minutes before their door had been locked. The first sign of it was a flag of truce which was borne up the northern road, with Coxo himself behind it.

By this time, the fighting on the road had died down, but it was raging bitterly to westward, as far down as the river bank, the invaders struggling to keep their way of retreat clear, and those who fought to free their own land striving to hem them in.

Lemno said: "There is sense in that. But I would give much to hear what he says. Will he get a truce?"

Gleda answered doubtfully: "It is not easy to guess. Amek has always talked of what he would do in a great war, which we had not expected to see. We had believed that wars were done."

"Well, we shall soon know."

Gleda said: "It seems that Coxo has got his will."

The noise of conflict had ceased, and there were no longer violent movements of men. It might be inferred that Coxo had not been delayed in getting the ear of whoever commanded—Amek himself, probably.

Lemno was easy—perhaps too easy—in mind. "There are several angles," he thought, "from which we who are together here can affect matters. We are an interesting quartet."

Meanwhile Coxo had been led to a white pavilion which had been pitched for Amek very near to his front line.

Coxo saw a trestle table, which was narrow and long, covered with a brown cloth, embroidered with crimson thread. The king sat midway of its length, so that Coxo and he were divided by no more than a narrow space.

The king asked: "You are one who controls? You are next to him? What do you ask? You would have a truce? Well, so you shall. It will be dark in less than two hours. You can have truce till dawn. We will all stay where we are. But you will not use the canoes during the night, either to remove spoil, or to bring men to your aid. That is agreed? Then I will give orders that men shall lay down their bows."

When he had done this, he said: "You are not feeding as we. You will welcome meat. Give our guest a stool."

So Coxo sat down opposite to the king. If he had doubted Gleda's tale before, he believed it now. Amek had the same steady eyes, beneath wide brows: the same mouth, and the cleft chin. He seemed younger than she, but he had an affirmative aspect of youth; impulsive, buoyant. Certainly, he would enjoy being king.

When Coxo's platter was ready, he said: "Time is short. We can talk and eat. Tell me why you have come?"

"I came to offer that we will withdraw, taking no spoil, if we may do so in peaceful paths."

"And how far would you do that?"

It was not a question that Coxo had expected to hear. But he did not hesitate in reply: "We would go back to our own homes." (If they should alter their minds and halt in the spiders' land, who could prevent that?)

Accepting the reply without comment, Amek asked: "And what compensation would be ours for the losses we have sustained? For dead men, and trampled garths, and disordered homes?"

"What could we do? We came because we are starving men. We must go back to starve."

"Unless you should conquer the spiders' land?"

"It would seem that you know a great deal."

"So I should. Ignorance makes a poor king."

"Yet I should say that there is one thing that you do not know."

145

"There are more than that. But our words stray. There must be retribution, though I may not be in a merciless mood. I will slay one man in ten, who shall be chosen by lot: or else you."

"But I came under flag of truce."

"So you did. And you shall go back with a neck that breathes. But I meant this: I can slay one in ten, or one in two, as I will, for I have you caught in a trap which you cannot break. Am I not informed of how few you are? And have you boats enough, even for them?

"But I give you a chance to save many lives. If you will die for all, I will call it enough."

"Why should I do that?"

"Because you lead. It is through you that they lie trapped as they are. And do you think my people would be content should I slay one only, if he were a poor kind?"

"But there is one who is over me."

"You mean Mendrale? Well, I do not say that I would refuse him. Would he be one to consent?"

"Can I speak for him in so great a thing? But there is one who is more than we, with whom you should be content."

Coxo felt that he had been nimble of wit to think of Lemno in this way, for it was far other than he had planned. He must readjust all. It was hard on him. It was changing front while the arrows fell.

Amek asked: "Who is he?"

"It is Lemno, who is over both (I am only third). He remained in the spiders' land, but he has now come over to take control, having heard that things did not go well with us. He is in our camp now."

"If he be willing to die, I will be content. But you made war without warning or cause, and it is the least that can be. You can go back now, and I must have this Lemno before the dawn, or you can count that you will all be in our pots, though there will be some we shall have to keep for a time, lest our bellies burst."

Amek laughed at this, and looked at Coxo as though he expected him to join in the mirth, which, weakly, he did.

The interview had not gone as he had meant it at all. He had intended to bargain for Gleda, one way or the other. But now he felt that it would be more prudent to leave her unmentioned, at least till there had been time for thought, and perhaps to find how the present proposal would do.

He took leave of a king who seemed to be in a merry mood, and went back to report to Mendrale.

CHAPTER XXXIX.

A QUESTION OF WHO SHALL DIE

MENDRALE said: "Couldn't you get him to talk seriously?"

"I don't think he was joking. He said he would be content with one, if he were at the top of the lot."

"I suppose the second in command wouldn't have been any use?" Mendrale asked, with a sneer in his voice.

"I hope not, because that would be you."

Mendrale stared at this, and Coxo, after a moment of silent enjoyment of his own joke, added: "I told him Lemno was boss, and that he had just come over to take control."

Mendrale looked almost apologetic. He might have known that Coxo would find some way of escape! But such consideration for himself was more than he would have hoped. Relief came, but was followed by doubt.

"He won't agree to that," he said definitely.

"You never know what Lemno might do."

They looked at one another in anxious speculation. Neither was sure that Lemno would not give his life to save a large number of men, if the issue were direct and simple. But he was not the leader for whom Amek had asked. How would they get over that? Could they expect him to accept Coxo's lie?

"It is a matter of how we put it to him," Mendrale said. "Perhaps you had better do that."

"Yes. Perhaps I had."

Coxo gave orders that Lemno's door should be quietly loosed on the outside, in the hope that he had not discovered what had been done before, and that a messenger should then request that he confer with Coxo on the floor below, to which Lemno readily gave assent.

He went down to the room where they had met before. Mendrale was absent. Coxo told his tale, using truth as far as it would avail, and lying glibly when there was nothing else to be done.

"He seemed to know everything," he said. "He knew that you had been making war in the spiders' land, and he knew you had come over to us. He assumed that you were supreme, and that you had come because you were not satisfied with what we had done."

"You could have told him that that was wrong."

"So I did. He would not believe it. He offered terms which, he said, were easy for us, but I cannot suppose that you will look at them in the same way."

"He wants his foot in my land?"

"He said nothing of that. He said if we would give you up we could go free."

"It is about Gleda?"

"I cannot say. She was not mentioned at all. Should I have been likely to speak of that which would fan his wrath?"

"It is a strange tale. I must talk of it with her."

"Well, you can do that. But if you are not in their camp before dawn we shall be lost men. As to Gleda, if you will take wisdom from me, you will say nothing to Amek of her, for it might be no welcome tale that she is now wedded to you. It might destroy the hope of moderate treatment which you would otherwise have; and how you took her first, though it might be of less moment to him, would not be that which a subject would approve, or a brother bless."

"There are many times," Lemno replied tonelessly, "when silence may be more helpful than speech; and I must thank the care which you show for me."

He went back to a room which was lighted now, and where he found the three he had left grouped around one of the windows, discussing its height from the ground, and things that might be done in the dark.

CHAPTER XL.

Coxo Sets Out Again

LEMNO spoke without reserve, letting the two men who were with them hear everything. He said: "Coxo has come back with a tale which cannot be wholly false, and may be almost entirely true; but I don't like it.

"He says that the truce will endure till dawn, and that there will then be peace, if only I shall have surrendered myself to Amek, for him to deal with me as he will, as having been the front of offence."

"That is silly," Gleda said. "I should call it a lie."

"But it must be less simple than that, or it would be a lie of small profit for him."

"Then it is the fruit of lies. That is easy to see."

"Perhaps. But could you guess what the lies were?"

"Why should Amek want you? I should ask that first."

"Coxo says that Amek thought I was first in command. He says he denied it, but was not believed."

Gleda saw that this, true or false, had a plausible sound; but, if it were true, it was a danger to Lemno which she only might be able to turn aside. She asked: "It might be your death, if we should not move in the right way. Had he heard of me?"

"He says he did not risk anything which might have made Amek more hostile to me, owing to how you were seized."

"That is a clear lie. It could have done you no harm at all, but a great good."

"That is what you should judge more surely than I."

"Will you go?"

"I think I must, for it seems that the bargain is plain. The men must be saved. But what Amek may be planning to do to me (on which Coxo could have been more clear than he was) is more hard to guess."

149

Gleda made no answer to that, and they fell to silence, both having reservations in their own minds. For Gleda thought that he should not go to such peril without her intercession, and he thought that he would not bring her name into it unless he could be sure that Amek would be her friend—Amek, who sat on a throne which was not his.

It was within the next hour that Amek—who was not destined to sleep much that night—was roused and told that Coxo sued for hearing again, on a matter which would not wait.

Amek rose on light and most ready feet. He thought: "This will be the thing he told me I did not know. Shall I know it now? I shall know what he says it is. And a good liar is always pleasant to hear."

He said: "Give him the drink that is due to an honoured guest. Tell him he shall be seen in a little time." He started combing his hair.

CHAPTER XLI.

COXO TALKS WELL

COXO said: "There was a matter which I would have mentioned before, but you put it firmly aside. I have thought more, and have talked to Mendrale thereon, and we are agreed that you must know, if we are to act in loyal friendship to you, as we both desire. It concerns one whom you thought drowned, who is Lemno's wife."

If there were a flicker of astonishment, or any other emotion, in Amek's eyes, it was so momentary that it left Coxo in doubt of what, if anything, it might imply; and after that a sphinx could not have been more blank-faced.

"You have decided well. Tell me all."

It was a disconcerting reply, disclosing nothing either of what Amek might already know, or of what his feelings might be. Coxo saw that he must take some steps in the dark, and he used the caution which that mode of progression requires. He said: "In a sense, it is not our matter at all. Lemno did not consult us when he caught your princess, thinking that she would make a good meal for a starving man, nor when he changed his mind, treating his own wife in a butcher's way (which may tell you of what kind he is), and putting the one he had caught in the vacant place. Nor was his bringing her back to this land a matter on which he would have held consultation with us, or which you could blame us for.

"But if he come to you before dawn, as you have required, whether on his feet, or at the end of a rope, and you slay him, as you have said, the princess will be in our hands, and we would like to know what we should do with her."

Amek asked: "Where is she now?"

"Lord, she is with Lemno."

"She is free to move? She is in no way constrained?"

Coxo paused. "That," he said at last, "is for Lemno to say. She is in his room."

151

"He is free to move as he will?"

"Lord, he is chief of all."

"So he may be. Yet you talked of his being brought at a rope's end."

"That would be if he should resist your will."

"I will ask you again, and I would have a most careful reply: is the princess free to move as she will?"

"Lord, it is not easy to say. She is not guarded or tied. But she has been little seen. And he is a man of blood. His first wife—"

"So you said before. Tell me this: when she came with him yesterday, was she free then?"

"Lord, I have been at the front of war. When he came, he called Mendrale and me to confer with him. She was in an upper room alone. She is still there. Can I say more?"

Amek looked at him in such a way that he felt he had said something wrong, though he could not guess what. He thought he had spoken truth at a low price. Then Amek said: "But you went over to him."

How could he have known that?

"Lord, I went in haste, being called by him. He was distant. I toiled through the night. When I found him, we had no more than a few words, after which he sent me back without rest to tell Mendrale that he would be here in the next hour after myself. I have had no rest at all."

Amek looked at him with attention. He certainly appeared to be a tired, as well as a much-worried man. He said: "I accept that."

Coxo felt that he had escaped well. He had not said whether he had seen Gleda on that occasion or not, and had not been asked. But he had seen that even a small lie could be a very dangerous thing.

Seeing him silent, Amek asked: "Have you more to say?"

"Lord, I have asked: if you have Lemno, and she be left with us, shall we take her back?"

"If Lemno be surrendered to me, I have pledged my word that you shall all have a free return. Does that cover any who are of this land? You can ask yourself. There is no more to be said. You should have some sleep, which you need." With these words Amek rose and went back to his bed-chamber.

Coxo had been agile of wit and discreet of speech. Yet exhaustion and loss of sleep may reduce physical alertness beyond the control of the strongest will, and it may be that, had he toiled less, he would not have failed, as he slogged wearily back, to see one who came toward him, and then turned, and leaped over the roadside fence.

152

Later, he was overtaken by one whom Amek had sent. "I bring you," he said, "a word from the king, which he says you will understand. At moonrise (which is two hours from now, being near the dawn), he will send escort, which will not be for one. It must be for two."

Having given this message, the man went, not waiting reply.

When Coxo got back to Mendrale, he said: "We shall not need to persuade Lemno to go on his free legs. Amek will be sending for him, and for the woman also. We shall be rid of both without blame; and we can do what we will in the spiders' land."

CHAPTER XLII.

AMEK IS WAKED AGAIN

AMEK said: "Am I not to rest at all? Let the man stew till the dawn."

"Lord, he was most urgent that he should not be put aside. He said that when you have heard him, you will give him thanks."

"Well, I will come out. Bid him wait."

Amek combed his hair for the second time before dawn, for he would not be seen by any in such guise as would be unseemly in one who ruled.

He came out looking alert, though he had yawned before moving the curtain aside, and he saw one of those whom Gleda had saved, he with the sound legs, who had been chosen to drop twelve feet to the ground, and to come by a back road.

He told his tale, as he had been instructed, and Amek listened until it was done, saying nothing, but heeding all, as a king should.

The man ended: "Lord, I was to say that they will both be here before dawn, but they would have you know these things first; and when they come they may have other things to say which will be pleasing to you."

"So they have planned to come here together? It would seem that we have been of the same mind," the king answered, so that those who heard could not tell whether he were pleased or no. Then he said: "I am about to ask you some things which should be answered with care, for they may be of more moment than you would guess. By whose word was it that your lives were saved at the last?"

"Lord, it was Coxo's order which cut our bonds, but I would not say—"

"You have said. As to this Lemno, did he seem to control all?"

The man appeared to find reply difficult. He said, after a pause: "Lord, he seemed neither to rule, nor as one ruled."

"And—my sister? Was she under duress from him? Did she move freely about?"

"She is in no fear of him. There was the time when the door held. That was equal for all."

"It tells much."

Amek dismissed him with no more words.

It was no long time after this that he was told that Lemno and Gleda were seeking audience of him.

He gave orders which caused some bustle without, and then said that Lemno should be brought in alone, "and heed well that he is not armed, and there must be with him sufficient guard, for he may be a dangerous man. But yet let it not be done as though he be a man in bondage to us. You will tell Her Highness that we have little of comfort here, but she shall have the best that there is, and we will meet within the hour, when I shall be more clear of affairs."

Lemno and Gleda stood together in the outer pavilion, having been brought to that point, and there stayed. The men who stood round them would not have found it easy to say whether they were escort or guard.

They knew Gleda, who a short fortnight before they would have hailed as their natural queen. They knew Lemno as one who was great in his own land, who was to have been brought for a shameful death, but who had come of his own will. His looks were not simple to read, but they were not those of a man who was resigned to being slain in the next hour. They saw a matter too great for them to resolve, and leaned on their halberds with watchful eyes.

The two who were so guarded heard the message, and could not call it either evil or good. Amek did not come out with stretched hands, as a brother should to greet a sister he had thought drowned, but he said she was to be served well. He would see Lemno alone, which might be well, or it might be that he would speak words which his sister, as Lemno's wife, should not hear. He might intend to give orders for Lemno to die at once, and then face her with the accomplished fact.

Gleda spoke with a quiet decision, half meant for the ears of those who were standing about: "I shall expect you in a very short time, or I shall come where you are. I am not to be put aside."

She felt confident, being among her own people, and Amek being one she had never feared.

Lemno said: "There is no cause to fret. If he talk, so can I."

In his thought was recollection of the old words he had read: *Power corrupts*. But, surely, that was not always true? Was there not one who had made the earth? And perhaps much beyond that? *Abso-*

lute power corrupts absolutely. To believe that must be to lose faith in all fundamental, in all ultimate things.

He did not wait for Amek to speak. Being brought to his presence, he was prompt to have the first word. He said, as addressing one who was no higher than he: "You are the brother, as I am told, of one I have made my wife. If you are as she, we should accord well."

He met hostile eyes. "You are the head of those who have spoiled our land, for which death must pay. Did she approve that?"

"It is false. I should say that Coxo told you that tale."

"So he did; and it had a most likely sound."

"He told me he had denied it to you, but you would not heed."

"I could believe that. Or else not. Will you tell me another thing? How did Gleda come to your bed?"

"I took her first for the pot, not knowing the rank she had. We were starving men."

"And your mind changed, so that she became a wife without choice?"

"Not at all. I had the offer from her."

"But if she had not professed to be of that mind?"

"How can I say? But it is a tale you should hear from her. She is held without, as she should not be."

"Then you can tell her that she can come here, and it is you who will wait without."

"I will do that. For it is well that you should see her alone." Lemno turned as he said that, and passed out, disregarding those who had led him in. They, having heard what was said, looked to Amek with doubtful eyes, and, getting no sign from him, they did nothing, which must have been what he had meant.

Lemno found some satisfaction from this freedom of movement, which would hardly have been allowed to one on the edge of death, though there had been little friendship in Amek's words. He said to Gleda, in a voice too low to be heard by those who stood round: "You are permitted to go in. He is somewhat on his hind legs, and unsure what the truth may be. But I should say you will have little trouble with him."

She said: "Oh, I may live!" with a note of laughter pleasant to hear, and passed into the inner pavilion, leaving him for a longer time than he had left her.

He had time to reflect that his life was in her hands, as hers had once been in his. Would she throw his away as lightly as he would have taken hers? He was assured that she would not, yet the thought caused him to look round for a halberd that might be loosely held, so that it might be snatched from the grasp of a careless man. So the time went by, until there was a faint gray prospect of dawn, which could be seen where the outer tent-flap was buckled back.

A man, having the aspect of one in a high command, came in from the road. He said to another, more or less of his kind: "I have made open the way. You may tell the king they are moving now."

The man answered: "It must wait. The Lady Gleda is with the king."

Lemno understood that the return of the frustrated army had begun. He thought he knew of two men who would be in the first canoes and, when they got to the other side, would lose no time in making mischief for him. He was wrong. For, as he was becoming weary of waiting for the end of what seemed to be an interminable interview, his attention was diverted by the entrance of Mendrale and Coxo, with a show of halberds around them which might be recognition of the greatness which had been theirs, but could be interpreted in a worse way.

Amek must have heard the bustle their entrance made, for a gong sounded within, and when an usher went to enquire what the king would have, he said: "You will ask Lemno to return, with the two who have just been brought in.

As they entered, the inner pavilion, though spacious, became so crowded that some guards, who would have followed, must stay without, and some others were crowded back somewhat into the king's bedchamber, looking on through its back-thonged flap.

The king sat at the long table, in the central seat he had held before, and Gleda was at his right hand. There was gravity in their eyes.

The king said to Lemno: "I kept you long awaiting. But I would have all start equal."

Mendrale was next to speak, losing no time: "Lord, I must protest that I have been brought here by duress, in violation of treaty made, which had been fulfilled on our side."

Amek said: "Are you sure of that? Then you walk a safe way, for I am of straight speech. Will you say the same of Coxo?"

Coxo felt many eyes were on him.

He said boldly: "So he may. I was as straight of speech as a man could be."

"Then you should have no fear of a butcher's knife."

Coxo disliked the tone of that, but he still showed a bold front. He said: "I have no reason to fear."

Amek went on: "I will ask you this: if you lied to me when you said that Lemno was in control here, and Mendrale was the name that you should have said, will you object if I put the knife to the right neck?"

"Lord," Mendrale broke in, his voice trembling with mingled indignation and fear, "I had no part in this, either by word or the written scroll. Shall I be brought to a shameful death for that which I did not do?"

"Surely not," Amek replied. "You will have no such injustice from me. But you knew the terms I had made, and that you were he whom I aimed to have. You have released those whom you led, and you have bought your death, as agreed. But for Coxo there must be a different judgment. For, were he second or third, it is clear that he was not first. I did not bargain for him. My faith is pledged that I let him go.

"But it was against Lemno he schemed, and—as I think—he had a slanting eye on my sister's life. What shall be his wage must be theirs to say."

Lemno saw that judgment must come from his mouth, which is the burden of power. He thought that, whether his own mood, in that hour of relief and gain, might be for mercy or wrath, it would be a poor gift to his land to let Coxo live. He looked to Gleda, who had known before what would be said, and she understood, and gave a reply which she had prepared before: "I think nothing of what he would have contrived for me. I was always beyond his reach. But he would have brought you to a shameful death by a cunning lie. There can be no mercy for that. Let him go to death by the same road."

"I think alike," Lemno replied. "He is not one for whom death should be kept waiting beyond the next hour. He should be slaughtered by common men, and his flesh be for those of the meanest sort. But for Mendrale I will ask this mercy, if"—he turned to Amek—"you will so allow. Let Mendrale give us a merry meal, for we have come to a time when we may rejoice together, and he is one who has been formed by nature to fill the pots for a kingly feast."

"That," Amek replied, "is a good thought. It shall be as you will. Mendrale shall thank you for that on his bent knees."

So, in fact, Mendrale would have been ready to do, but at that moment a breathless messenger burst without ceremony into the tent.

"Lord," he cried, "a spider has landed, and comes this way!"

CHAPTER XLIII.

ONE SPIDER

FOR a short distance most spiders can run fast. The hunting spiders, who do not make webs, but must ambush or chase their prey, can do a short distance so swiftly that few creatures of their own size can keep the space ahead that their lives require.

The spider which had interrupted Amek's judgments had come down the road with no object of pursuit. He was urged by fear.

He had been chasing a man in his own land who had come to the river shore just as a laden canoe had pulled in. At the sight of the monstrous form, which was strange to them, the men in the canoe cast off in panic; and as they did so the hunted man leaped aboard. It was a leap which passed over eight feet of water that each second made more—and two seconds later the spider followed.

The distance was nothing to him, but he came down with only two of his eight legs upon a canoe which wobbled and swerved, and with the rest of them in a swift current.

The men paddled frantically while, by the way in which they shrank away from the struggling green horror, they helped to balance the canoe against the pull of the spider's body, half above the water, amid waving legs. By luck or by miracle they came to the farther bank, by which time the half-drowned creature had forgotten even his perennial hunger in terror which was quickly translated into panic flight.

Seeing a straight fenced road, wide enough for his body to pass, he had rushed along it for half a mile. Soon he became aware both of muscular exhaustion and the absence of any reason for further fear.

Now he moved on sedately, feeling the roadside fences with sensitive legs, or reaching over them to explore the thickness of the underbrush which retarded him from the course which he would have preferred to take.

Meanwhile Lemno was saying: "If he be only one, he should be soon dead, you having so many bow-men here. But we shall be safe here in the thicker trees."

This was said as they left the pavilion, to find no spider in sight, but confirmation of what they had heard in a confusion of running and shouting men, who checked somewhat and quietened in the presence of their king, finding that he surveyed them with merry and contemptuous eyes.

"If," he said, in a voice which was rather boyish of tone, but carried far, "you do not welcome a spider here, you should face his way and give him cause to return or to lie still. Let those with bows fall into one rank, and they shall be told how this game is played."

He turned to Lemno to say: "If you will take charge of this, you will have my thanks, for you know best. But I will not ask you to take a danger I do not share."

As he said this, a man came out from the trees. He cried: "Lord, the spider is on the high road. It stands still."

Lemno addressed the bowmen, telling them how they should shoot when they had got close under the trees, but keeping far enough away to be out of the creature's reach. Then he took a halberd, which he saw to be a better weapon than a poker, and the king did the same. He chose a score of good men who had the same weapons in hand, and they went to where the great beast had halted, standing so absolutely still that it might be thought that he was dead on his legs.

So he remained, motionless, while the bowmen took up their positions on both his sides, and also somewhat behind for a slanting shot, but with none in front, that they might not be seen by eyes which must look ahead.

But the spider did not depend on his eyes. He had more detailed reports than they could have given, running up each sensitive, flexible leg. He was aware of every spot where a man lay.

Suddenly, just as the bows drew, he was gone. With no preliminary movements, the immobility changed to an instant rush up the trees, over the tops of which he fled, beyond observation, and deriding the idea of pursuit.

The sudden movement interrupted the details which Lemno was giving concerning its curious anatomy, to a king who was more interested to learn than concerned for any peril which there might be.

It was three weeks before that spider was brought to death, during which time it sucked the living juices of some pigs, and two men; but there was much to happen before that day.

160

CHAPTER XLIV.

Flight

AMEK had some kingly qualities, but he was young, and the excitement of hearing that one of the giant green spiders, which had been near fable to him, was at his door, had chased other things from his mind.

His men had been excited too, and had followed his lead. But Mendrale and Coxo had had more urgent matters upon their minds. With attention diverted for a moment from them, they had slipped into the trees, and made good speed to the river side, where they came to a crowded bank.

It must, under the circumstances of which they already knew, have been a place of traffic and noise. They expected that; but not what they saw.

There were many scores of their men who had come there seeking transportation as rapidly as the canoes could take them away; and there was a company that Amek had sent to watch that no booty should be removed.

But though the canoes had made one journey, they had returned fuller than they had gone, for as the men had jumped out, others with more eagerness had jumped in, and when these men had landed and told their tale, there were few who did not wish to remain where they then were, at least until darkness should give them freedom to cross the peninsula without fear and so go on to their own land.

For the defeat of the spiders had not ended the war. It had not even discouraged them. On the contrary, it appeared to have aroused them to angry consciousness of the attack which was being made upon them, and, for the first time, they had reacted with all their strength.

Many hundreds of spiders—possibly all there were, excepting those in a condition of skin-shedding, which would render them unfit for action—had advanced in one large concerted movement, covering the whole width of the narrowing peninsula, evidently intending to make systematic destruction of the invading pest.

The path along the river bank had been blocked immediately, and was being cleared and widened sufficiently for the spiders to use it as an outflanking alley, from which they could penetrate at any favourable point, to surround an area which they could then reduce at leisure.

Working forward from the scene of their defeat, to which they had quickly returned, they had, on the first day, isolated a party of about thirty who had held their ground in a thick clump of trees, where the undergrowth was dense, without giving sufficient heed to the fact that it was sparse both to right and left; and before evening came they had been patrolling the tops of the trees with a vigilance which allowed no relaxation of caution to any who were below, and making sudden descents wherever their bodies could move, and their palpi penetrate beneath the cover.

There would have been a larger exodus during the night but for the fact that the canoes were all on the farther bank. As it was, a large number who could swim sufficiently well to be undeterred by the swiftness of the current of the upper river had left before morning came, preferring the certainty of famine in their own peaceful land to the close hazard of death where the spiders swarmed.

Lemno questioned one of those who had fled in the canoe which towed the spider across the river.

He was aware of Amek standing beside him, with an amusement in his eyes which was no less hard to endure because it was not malicious. Here was a different picture from that which he had drawn in good faith a short time before!

He said to the man: "It seems that much has happened in a few hours. Did Relf give you orders to run?"

The man answered with some indignation: "I was not one who ran, till an hour ago. What else can a man do when a spider's palp is feeling for him three yards away? As to Relf, he has given orders to none since yesterday. It is likely that he is dead, but there are those who say that he is cut off near the western bank, where the spiders cut a swathe through the trees, as it is a marvel to see them do."

"I have seen something of that," Lemno answered, mollified. "And I can see also that I was called away at an unfortunate hour. If Relf be so caught, we must help. Has there been much loss besides that? Is Plera with Relf? Is Jalna still using a deadly bow?"

"I saw nothing of them," the man replied, "but it is a likely guess. And as for the bows, they were thrown aside, for no arrows were left. Being driven back, as we were, a shaft loosed was a shaft lost, even though it might fall wide of its mark."

"I can see," Lemno said, "that we have to begin again, and perhaps by a harder way than we had before. But you must not think that we shall abandon Relf, or leave the spiders to rule the land."

"You have one gain," Amek remarked, with an appraisal which was sanguine and yet shrewd, "that you have not to seek the spiders farther away. They have come to you, and, I should guess, with all the force that they have."

"Amek," Gleda broke in, "when I said that I should ask nothing further of you if Lemno should come free, I meant it without reserve. But this I did not foresee. Will you hold me to that now?"

"No. You may ask and have, as I know you would deal with me."

"Then I will have a thousand of the best men that you can array. And five hundred extra bows, and enough arrows, and any halberds which we may need. And food without stint (but you promised that), which you can well spare."

"You can have it all. But one bargain. That Lemno will let me come with you; for this is a better war than that we leave behind."

Lemno said: "I thank you. And, though I might not have asked so much, I do not say that we shall not need everything Gleda has said."

"You will need them all, as I see it," Amek replied, "and at all the speed we can make."

There was reason in what he said, for they were divided by no more than the river's breadth from a scene of death which, from here, they could do nothing to aid.

Those of Lemno's men who would have escaped during the night, had canoes been there, were assembled thickly. The spiders had advanced upon these in a long line, leaping down from the trees in hundreds at once. To gain the shelter of the forest, it was necessary to dodge backward between them, as many did, and some succeeded, while others died. Some, with sufficient courage or desperation to stand their ground, did what damage they could with poker or scythe to their monstrous foes. Those who had lost heart came running to the water's edge, screaming for canoes to come and take them away.

It was a scene of carnage and defeat which was hard to watch, for the spiders no longer stopped to suck the juice of a captured foe. They slew, and hurried forward, and slew again.

Amek said to Lemno: "What shall be done? It is for you to say."

Lemno said: "We will load the canoes with the best men here, taking many bows, and land higher up, under the trees. The canoes can then drop down the river (it will not be far), and load up those who are now howling to go, and bring them up to where we shall be. But I will have none returned either to this side or the land they left. They would be in a flight which I will not have."

"There are some who are born to lead," Amek replied, at which Gleda was pleased.

She said: "It is those who are of a like mind who are quick to see," at which those who heard were also content; and while they talked they descended the bank to the canoes, not knowing in which direction movement would be.

CHAPTER XLV.

RALLY

GLEDA got into the first canoe as one who took a place which was rightly hers, and Lemno made no objection. She might not be good for a halberd's thrust, nor skilled with a bow, but it was an example of courage and coolness which was required.

"You will pardon me if I do not speak," he said to Amek as they embarked, "for I am anxious to get into contact with Relf, from whom I should obtain information which it is vital for us to have. I tried as soon as I saw the disaster which has occurred, but got no response."

He remained abstracted during the short time that they were crossing the river, and for some minutes beyond that, Amek watching him curiously, for though he would have said (with some truth) that his people were of higher civilization in other ways, they had not developed this use of telepathy to the same point. He saw that Gleda was watching Lemno as one waiting to speak, and when he made a gesture of resignation, saying: "I suppose he is dead," she broke in at once with: "Had you been less fixed on that which you cannot get, you would have known that Jalna is seeking you."

At which, without making reply, he lapsed into abstraction again, while Amek asked Gleda: "Can you tell me what you learned?"

"I can tell you this, which is all that I had from her, for it is Lemno in whom she thinks that her rescue lies. There are twenty-three alive of those trapped. Some are hurt, and all starve. Relf has a broken head, and his wits are gone. The spiders are round them on every side, mowing down trees—"

"Can they do that?"

"I have seen it done. They make ropes of silk, which are thin, and yet of unbelievable strength. The spiders cast the cord round a group of trees, be they large or small, and the trees are cut through when they pull on the rope; or, more often, their roots come up, and they are dragged flat."

So it was. As rats or rabbits may hide in the last central patch of the standing corn, while the blades go round it, and reduce the shelter which it provides, so did the twenty-three men and women, nursing wounds, and without water or food, withdraw to a centre into which the light penetrated with increasing strength, as the spiders, while appearing to ignore their existence, drew their narrowing circles round it.

That was the picture Jalna gave, to which Lemno replied with the assurance she required. "Tell them all," was his message, "that we are crossing the river now, and they may expect that the spiders will soon cease to surround them, for we shall give them other matters of which to think." It was only when he felt that he had put some of his own confidence into her terrified mind that he cut off the connection.

"The approach," he said to Amek, "we had cleared along the west bank is now in the spiders' hands. The narrow tracks which we had beaten through the woods to the cleared space cannot be reached, while the end of the peninsula, from which they start, is overrun by spiders. As I see it, we can do no better than to make straight for our goal."

"I am sure," Amek replied, "that it is a matter which you are best fitted to judge. But I have one question to ask: where the undergrowth is dense, it must be protection to you, but, to the same degree, it delays your pace. Could you not make better speed through the trees, and with safety enough, taking them at their midst, neither high nor low?"

"I have had the same thought," Lemno replied, "for the conditions are varied from what they were. At our first attempt, we knew less of what the degree of danger might be, and we aimed to be secret in all we did.

"Now, the sooner they know of our advance, the better it may be for those who are closely pressed, and speed has become of more account than it was then. It has added dangers—in particular that they can prepare defense at any open space where they will see that it is our purpose to cross; but, even so, we can swerve aside as far as we will.

"What I plan is that we shall advance through the trees, one man of mine, from those who will be brought here from below, being attached to every ten of yours, or those who were with Mendrale before, and that they will descend to the ground when they come near to the place where the spiders are working. I will go with the first ten, for I shall have guidance from Jalna of where they are."

"And I will be at your side."

"That were surely unwise, for we might both fall into one snare."

"Would you have me lurk in a safe rear? It is asking much."

"Yet it might be the wiser way. But if you would be more ahead, I will go on the right hand, and you can take the left. You will have control there, and I will have an order issued that, if I be trapped or dead, they shall be led by you."

"That is the word of a friend. But I have a bargain with Gleda that only she can be second to you in this land; I come here as one who will leave when it is won."

"Then we will ask her assent, which should be easy to have."

But when they turned to Gleda, who had lain down at this pause; she was in a sleep which they would not break.

The ground was cold and a fine rain was beginning to fall, being a sure sign that the winter neared, but she had obtained some garments such as were native to her, which had been left in the dwellings of those who had fled. Over these she had wrapped the fur cloak which was still warm, though scratched and torn and befouled; and she slept dry.

Amek said: "I suppose that she had no sleep last night. Shall we wake her? I should say not."

"And I say the same for another reason. If she wake, she will want to come with me. She is better here."

"Yet if the spiders see us?"

"So they may. But, should they come, she will have had warning enough. She will not sleep through the noise. And she is aware of what the spiders can do—and where safety lies."

CHAPTER XLVI.

The Fate of Mendrale

THE men among whom Mendrale and Coxo came had no cause to regard them as other than their natural leaders, and the company which Amek had sent had no orders except to watch that goods should not be ferried away. They could have taken control, if they would, and how they would have acted had they found all going well, it is idle to ask.

They came to men who were of a doubtful mind as to what they should do, and whose doubts became less as each minute passed, and they were more resolved to stay where they were, at least till night.

But the two thought such a delay would be too great a hazard. They could both swim, and that was what they resolved to do. They could not go below the peninsula, for that was where the rivers joined, and the rapids began. They could not swim in the sight of all, to land on the open ground, where men clamoured to be taken off, and some spiders were raging there. They did what Lemno would arrange that all should do in the next hour. They went upstream; though not as far as the place where he would cross, and swam the river unseen of any spiders or men.

They penetrated the densest cover that they could find for the next hour, green spiders in the trees above coming more than once between them and the light, and then Coxo could do no more.

Mendrale had had no sleep during the past night, but Coxo's sleepless nights had been two. Also, he had exerted himself more, both in wits and legs. He lay down where the thickness of leaf and bough was not yet penetrated by the fine rain which had begun its descent, and in a moment he was asleep.

Mendrale looked at him, and his doubt was short. Whatever strength Coxo may have had at the first, he was now the weaker and wearier man. He was to be left. Mendrale went on alone.

168

He headed for the western river, and he would then only have to swim it—as he could easily do—to be in the security of his own land, where Amek would have no jurisdiction at all; and Lemno would not be a great fear, as he was unlikely to return, and, if he should, what was there but public opinion to dread? Even if Lemno should make a proofless wrong a matter of personal strife, Mendrale thought that he might be equal to saving himself. He went on, thinking that his troubles were nearly done.

In this mood, he finished crossing the peninsula (which was not very wide at that point) with exhausting toil, but no more alarm than came from the sight of a green bulk scurrying overhead, which once came between him and the sun. He arrived at the western bank, where he saw that the spiders were busy, widening the track which Lemno had made.

Mendrale stayed here for some time, waiting his chance. He saw that he must rush that narrow space only when no spider was near. He did not underestimate the speed at which they would come if he should be seen. But he had patience, and he chose his time well.

Only he did not heed the green silken cords, of which there were three lying loosely among the forest grasses and fallen leaves. As he touched one of these, it jumped to sudden tautness, and the speed with which he ran gave him the heavier fall. He had only re-gained his knees when the clawed palpi of a large female spider gripped him on either side of his neck. He could not see what lifted him, being unable to turn his head. He did not know that he was held up to the close inspection of eight expressionless, unwinking eyes. But he felt the stab of the poison-prong in his back, and screamed as it withdrew. He knew little beyond that, and was unconscious when the crushers closed upon his body from either side, and his juices were squeezed into the bony mouth.

CHAPTER XLVII.

SIEGE

THERE had been twenty men and three women who had found themselves too tightly cordoned to escape, as some of their comrades had done when the danger was first perceived.

Now there were twenty-two, for one lay dead. He had been torn by a spider's claw, and though the bleeding had been stopped at last, it had left him too weak to endure for more than a few hours.

The spider that had clawed him was also dead: a monstrous sight which they might regard with dread or satisfaction, but which they could not escape.

A half-grown female, in her lust for their lives, had pushed a way through the trees until she stuck fast, so that she had become easy to slay. And the place where she had died was now the very centre of the limited space of safety which still remained. She had died making no sound, but with vicious struggles that shook the trees, and threshing of many limbs. Now they could look up without fear, but not without horror, at the two rows of expressionless eyes in the front of the headless body. The outer joints of the limbs had been hacked and broken; the abdomen has been torn by many pokers, and much of its contents had spilled onto the ground, but, from the front, the deadly monster might have been still alive in its motionless, waiting way.

They had discussed eating it in their hunger, but repulsion had been too strong, and, even then, the need of water had become acute enough to render hunger a secondary matter.

By the time the injured man died, the desire for any food had receded before the more urgent need. Thirst was their only consciousness—thirst and fear. For, as the dawn had come, the steady, silent circuit of death resumed. With no direct regard for the existence of those whom they toiled to reach, the spiders continued to tear down the surrounding trees, and the oasis of safety narrowed from side to side.

But one relief came, when, an hour after the dawn, the rain fell thinly, but with a fine penetration that soaked dried skins and gave moisture to outthrust tongues.

It brought consciousness to Relf, by whose side Plera had sat sleeplessly all night, seeking with whispered words to reach the mind of one who made no reply, and feeling heart beats which became stronger and more regular as the hours passed.

Now Relf asked, in a stronger voice than she had expected to hear: "Are they round us still? Do they come close? I must reach Lemno, if I can, though there may be no hope from him. For what can he do from that land? Is there no water at all?"

"Lemno is nearing now," Plera replied. "He comes fast through the trees with a strong help. He may be in time. Even now, Jalna has been speaking to him."

Jalna, sitting near, confirmed this. She sat nursing two arrows which had been withdrawn from the carcass of the dead spider, all having agreed that they would be most useful with her. But neither these, nor the hope that Lemno would soon arrive, gave her confidence sufficient to rule her fears.

Relf saw her tremble at the sound of a great tree's fall, and said: "If you are to be the one to let fly, you must control fear. You must shoot with a steady hand."

"It will not shake when I shoot," she said bitterly. "There will be two dead. You can take assurance of that."

But of what avail, she thought, would that be?

Crawling under bushes, a man came from the edge of the little wood that was left to them. He said: "We have severed one of their ropes. The trees are close there, and they can pass them round no more than one or two at a time on our side. When they were set to pull, we crawled close, and burned the rope."

"That," Relf said, "should cause some delay. I will ask Lemno where he is now."

He was in communication with Lemno almost at once. He was asked: "Can you hold out for five hours from now? Some of us come through the trees, and some cut through below. Men follow in a stream which will flow till a thousand are here, or perhaps two. The spiders are swarming upon us from every side. They tear down through the trees, so that we cannot advance straight ahead. But we lose no time."

Relf answered: "We will hope to be here. But, be that as it may, we must give you thanks while our breaths last, for the toils and hazards that you endure. Maybe the spiders will slacken here, as they know you approach."

"Perhaps," Lemno replied, "but I should say they know everything now."

After that there was no change for a long time, with no sound but that of the falling trees, and but little said until Relf asked Jalna if she would not do better to use her arrows then, rather than wait for a worse need.

"For you must think," he said, "that if you kill one now there will be one less at the ropes; and, the earlier his death, the later the others will reach us."

Jalna could not deny that, but she had extreme reluctance to use those shafts, which, she felt, could still turn death aside at his first or second approach. She gave way at last, to the extent that she would use one now if she could have a sure shot, and keep the other for her own need, or until a sound of rescue should reach their ears.

On this bargain, she crept as near as she dared to the place where the spiders moved, and considered how she could be sure of a fatal shot.

As she looked out, a roped tree on her right with a high straight trunk bent toward her, as though borne down by a mighty wind. She watched the two strands of silken rope tauten before her and knew that it was of a great length, so that the spiders who pulled should be beyond the reach of the falling branches. She saw that, as the tree bent without breaking, the rope slipped somewhat up its slanting bole, and wondered how far that might continue, perhaps how the great trunk would spring back, and stand quivering in its escape from a dreadful death. And then, suddenly, it fell, with its roots thrown up to the air, and a high scatter of earth and stones.

The falling branches crashed past those of the trees under which she crouched, dragging some of them down, and forming a double curtain of leaf and bough, through which she could only see in a patchy way. But what she did see roused her to alertness, and to fix the shaft to a bended bow.

The tree having been uprooted, and the cord having slipped as far as it did, the spiders were grouping on the farther side to agree how it should be removed. Looking thus at the tree, they were facing her.

It must be a difficult shot, through obscuring leaves, and could be but an instant's chance. But the shaft leaped from the bow.

It sank deep into the eye of a spider who stood still for a minute's space, as though it had not been hurt at all. And then the hairy legs weakened, and the whole body collapsed among them.

172

Jalna's heart beat fast with excitement and pride. It had been a shot through the swaying leaves which had required almost miraculous luck—or skill. Could she never miss?

She wished she had further shafts to spare, for there were a dozen others around the slain spider now. Spiders that tore and sucked, showing that it was not a prerogative of mankind to know that there is no better food than a fellow's flesh.

She did not reflect that it also showed how confident they had become, for, in the stress of battle before, it was not what they had attempted to do. Yet the stress came, for, as they fed, a dozen huge females crowding around, and driving off the weaker males with a fierce warning which they were not foolish enough to ignore, other spiders came scrambling over the tops of the farther trees, at which, though there was no sound or sign of how communication was made, they drew back from gorging upon the dead, and for some minutes there was a general stillness, both among those who came, and those who were there before.

CHAPTER XLVIII.

THEY WAIT FOR DEATH

THE silent stillness ended after a time. The spiders who had come went away over the trees, a brighter green than the thinning leaves, shuffling over the branches with swift assurance on their many flexible legs, and those who had been busy with their cannibal feast returned to it again, but they were less numerous now. Some of those who had been pressing the siege must have joined those who withdrew. What could be the meaning of that?

As the next hour passed, they realized that the uprooting of trees had stopped. Those spiders who remained surrounded and watched, but they had ceased the work on which they had been active before. What could be the meaning of *that*?

They also noticed that, of those spiders who were still round them, most—indeed, all, except those who had resumed the feast—were the weaker males

Relf called on Lemno to report these things, and to consult as to what they might mean. Lemno said that the advance was becoming slower. It seemed as if all the spiders the land contained were assembling to bar their way.

Relf suggested that the attempt to destroy his isolated party was being deliberately delayed, because they were bait to draw the rescuing force in the direction which the spiders desired that it should come.

If that were so, Lemno replied, it meant that a decisive battle would be fought at once. But they saw, in exchanging a thought which rose together in both their minds, that the spiders would not intend to delay long enough to allow any rescue. If the front of battle should move too nearly, it might be the signal for fresh activity, and their swift destruction. Then Relf was conscious of a thought of encouragement from Lemno's mind, which ceased abruptly, before taking a concrete form. Had he seen a way in which that danger

174

could be rebuffed? And had he been too cautious to put it upon the air, in the unlikely fear that their weird opponents could tap their thoughts?

He must surmise that, if he would; but there was no further communication to be obtained. They must lie and wait.

The rain had ceased, but their thirst had been partly appeased, and consciousness of hunger became more acute. They made shift to start a fire under the narrow cover that remained, and cut up the man who had so conveniently died. They said to each other that it would be pleasure to him to know that he had not died entirely in vain.

So the afternoon passed, and the twilight came, the spiders still patrolling around them, with no effort to destroy their remaining cover. They heard no sound to indicate that the war was coming nearer to them, but there was little significance in that, for they knew that it was a silent one.

Jalna sat with the bow over her knees, and her fingers round the remaining shaft. She looked under the trees, and saw the movements of green, hairy legs as the spiders patrolled around. One of them will die, she thought—one of them will die. But after that—her hand trembled, and would not be still.

With the dusk, the rain came again, giving them some strength, and inclination to eat anew. They debated whether they should try to escape during the night, but it was not very dark, and the spiders, though they might be asleep on their legs, were close. They supposed that there would be snares of silken cords, very cunningly laid, and some of a glutinous kind, from which it would not be easy to break away.

They resolved to stay where they were, hoping that Lemno would come.

CHAPTER XLIX.

HOW THE SLEEPERS MET

GLEDA rose from a long sleep. She was refreshed, but not instantly alert. As she yawned, she saw men of her own land, men she knew, landing from the canoes.

Most of them carried axes, for which Amek had sent some hours before, preferring them to either halberds or knives. There were a few scythes also, which might be equally useful for cleaning thorns or for spilling a spider's belly upon the ground.

Gleda asked one who marshalled them how matters went, but she learned little. "Highness," he said, "we know nothing here, except that, as they land, the men go forward among the trees."

"They do not go through the upper boughs, as was ruled at first?"

"I cannot say."

She asked for food, which was quickly brought. She said that she would see for herself. She followed the axe men.

After a time, she saw a pig-path to the left of where the broad clearance had been made. It was one that she thought she knew. It did not go forward in the required direction, but, if she made a good guess, it was soon crossed by one that did. Being eager to join Lemno as promptly as possible, she thought that she would make use of it as far as she might, and then take to the upper boughs.

Her memory was correct, but she could not have foreseen that, as she turned into the northward path, she would face Coxo, ten yards away.

Coxo ran well. But there were those behind who ran as well, if not better than he.

He had a long knife in his hand, and he had no mind to be stopped by her, nor was she of a mood to meet him in single strife. She shrank as far aside as she could on the narrow path, and raised her poker to parry the knife.

But, as they met, she remembered that he had plotted against Lemno's life, which she could not forgive. And Lemno had said he should die. Slowly, tensely, she straightened.

He saw the threat of the poker, and his knife turned it adroitly away, but as he tried to run past her, he felt it between his legs, tripping him up.

He fell sprawling but unhurt. It was less the impulse to kill than fear of what the knife might do that gave strength to her lifted arm. The poker went in at his loins, and she leaned upon it until it entered the ground.

He might wriggle and scream, but there was no getting away from that, nor would it have been worth while to attempt, for his kidneys would be no more use to him, nor could they be roasted whole.

She was in no haste to pull the poker away, but did so as his pursuers came up, and she knew that no more need be feared from him.

"Highness," they said—for they were of her own men—"it was deftly done. We had not known you to be so great a woman of war."

"I am not that," she replied, "nor shall ever be. And I have done wrong, for he had been doomed to another death. But there was little time to decide. You can take him up for the kitchen now, but I should advise you to boil his legs."

CHAPTER L.

THE COMING OF NIGHT

LEAVING Coxo to benefit his fellow men in the only way that he would still be able to do, Gleda went northward again, and soon found cause to move with caution where battle raged, not on one continuous front, but in patches upon the ground, and many flurries amidst the leaves.

For the spiders probed down now at every opening among the trees, and encountered foes who no longer squirmed backward to the deepest cover, to watch for them with fearful eyes, but climbed up to meet them among the boughs.

The spiders reached downward, tearing great branches away that they might grip their foes, and the men struck upward with leaping shafts, and knife thrusts at close hand. Many died, but not only men, and the torn branches could not be cast aside, except onto the tops of surrounding trees, where they made better protection for those who fought from below.

But much of the fighting was on the ground, for the position was very different from what it had been. Now a spider who came down, even in a narrow place, would find no lack of out-bursting foes. Those they seized they killed. But meanwhile they must suffer wounds, from which they weakened until they died. Green blood soaked autumn grass of a duller hue. Green blood dripped through the trees.

It was a battle of ragged front and uncertain rear, leaderless now, so that it had become a simple question of which would give way the first, or endure till there should be none left for palpi or pike to slay.

Gleda did not seek to make war on the nearest spider. She sought Lemno. She supposed that he would be on the front of war, and that she would have a perilous passage to reach his side. She

178

had not heard the agreement that Lemno and Amek had made, that they would operate one on each flank, with Lemno upon the right.

Actually, she bore to the left, which was a fortunate error for her, for Lemno, after his last communication with Relf, had resolved upon a leftward operation, and had been moving across the front as rapidly as its condition allowed. Chance brought them nearly together, but she would not have seen him as she went directly ahead. More conspicuous herself among fighting men, she came to his notice, as his eyes searched all ways to learn how the fight went, and in a few moments he reached her side. She came sure-footed down a great branch of the tree she planned to cross, and as she gained its centre he dropped from a higher place.

"You are safe!" she said.

"What are you doing here?"

"My own place is with you; I was seeking it."

He said tonelessly, "Well, let us go on, taking ever the safer way. I am not looking for spiders to kill. I must find Amek."

So they went on together.

Finding Amek was no easy matter amid such confusion over so great a space, with strife raging invisibly in the boughs. But it was done before darkness came.

He rested with some companions under a tree, glad of the cooling rain, which fell on them as it fell on Relf at this time, and eating food which had been brought up from the rear.

For during the last hour half the new men who arrived had carried loads of water and food.

Amek, in spite of a bruised head and a side which was streaked with blood, was in merry mood.

"Sister," he said, "I owe you thanks for a crown, and for more than that. It is such a fight as I had not thought to see in my life's length."

Lemno, more sober of mood, described how the besieged company were placed, and their increasing jeopardy as relief approached. "Even," he said, "if we could reach them within an hour, there would be danger for them. And we have advanced little since noon. That is plain from the numbers of dead, both of spiders and ours, and all on a narrow line."

"So it may be," Amek replied, with unabated cheerfulness, "but there is the difference that we bring up fresh men all the time, while, if I guess right, the spiders are all here. It is a fight we must surely win, though I could wish it were at less cost."

"Perhaps," Lemno replied, "but I have a proposal which should bring relief to those in distress, and may reduce the spiders' courage.

Could we not get around their flank, at the river's edge, and relieve our friends from the rear?"

They debated this for some time. The spiders might not be on guard during the night, it being a movement they were unlikely to expect. This raised a further question of whether, should it have initial success, it might not be pressed on a larger scale. They discussed what the position might become if all reinforcements during the night or the next day should be diverted to that flank. Would the front line hold?—if line were the word to use for the confusion of conflict within the woods, which only darkness had lessened. Would they prevail at one point at the cost of disaster elsewhere? And what might follow from that?

In the end it was agreed that men who had marched or fought or hacked at undergrowth all through the day could not fight without rest all through the night and the day beyond. Food and sleep they must have.

So, as twilight fell, and the spiders relaxed their attack, orders were made that all should rest till three hours before dawn, at which time a hundred volunteers, well-armed men, with others behind bringing water and food, should attempt to turn the spiders' position by the route of the river bank; and that a further force, consisting largely of men who, having landed late, or who would do so during the night, would be unwearied and fit for war, should be marshalled to support any success which might be obtained. But the immediate object was to relieve those who had been cut off, to take them water and food, and to either strengthen their position, or bring them safely away.

It was Amek's assumption that he would be the leader of this expedition. Was it not an attack from the left flank, and was not that position clearly allotted to him? Lemno admitted this, but he was less willing that Gleda should go, as she said she must. Were not Plera and Jalna there? Might they not require services such as only she could supply? Lemno could not answer that, being vague as to what she might mean. He was more impressed by Amek's argument that it might be safer for her to go than to stay with him, for he would surely be at the front of the main battle at dawn.

So Gleda had her way, as a woman will. She lay with Lemno during the early hours of the night, of which both were glad, and, having had her own rest during the day, would have talked long, but she found that she lay by a weary man.

CHAPTER LI.

AMEK FINDS A WIFE

THE moon went down, but the sky cleared, showing stars, as they moved silently under the thick trees, searching the ground for the deadly cords which could give instant alarm.

But no hostile sound disturbed the stillness of the cool night. They could not move with less caution for that. There might be more cause for alarm in the freedom which had been left to them to advance as they would, than if they had been obstructed at every yard.

So they moved slowly under the trees, taking more time than had been foreseen, and the dawn had broadened before they looked out over the ashes of the great building which Lemno had burned, and what they saw roused them to wrath and haste.

For the trees fell—the last protections of those whom they sought to rescue were falling fast. Only the male spiders who had been left on the previous day could be seen, but they had started the final demolitions at the first light, that being part of the spiders' strategic plan, which Lemno and Relf had guessed correctly. But it had gone further than they expected.

It was true that the bait had been deliberately left, so that all effort and concentration might be directed to its relief, but the plan was not merely to draw the attackers forward. It had been designed to include a massed assault to be made upon Lemno's right flank at the dawn, which was to move down to capture the river bank, and so cut off the reinforcements which landed from the canoes.

The spiders had seen these landings of too-numerous foes, with no means of judging when they would end, or indeed, that they ever would. They had planned, with some strategic subtlety, to receive, isolate, and destroy a sufficient number to discourage further attempts to occupy their land. With this purpose they had made no effort to obstruct the landings during the first day, and had met the advance with no more than a token opposition, which they expected to

181

bring them victory very quickly when reinforcements should cease to arrive.

They may have failed to allow adequately for the additional numbers which would be landed during the night, or even overlooked this aspect entirely, not being used themselves to activity during the dark hours. But the plan was otherwise sound enough.

At the first glimmer of dawn, they had attacked both in front and flank, but most heavily on Lemno's right rear, so that he might be cut off from his base on the river bank.

There was advantage to them in this early hour, for men waked needing food, while the spiders' bodies were made in a better way. They had, in addition to the usual resources and accommodation for the digestion of food, what may be described as reserve tanks in their abdomens, where surplus juice was stored, to an extent which would make them independent of food for a month, if such need should be. This did not prevent them from always being eager to eat, for they hungered unless these tanks were entirely full.

And now, as they stirred from the immobility of the night, it was to instant action against their foes.

Jalna saw the trees crash, and their noise was a sound of doom. She looked at the hateful forms moving without, and said aloud: "I will kill one. One will die sooner than I." But she found little consolation in that.

She saw the men who crouched round her with knives and pokers, resolved also that they would not die by the fangs of unwounded foes, but she knew that they were too few to do more than defer their deaths for minutes rather than hours. And then the long-dreaded moment came.

She saw the last boughs dragged away from above her head. She looked up at eight confronting eyes.

She was conscious of the forward movement of hairy legs. She saw the palpi reaching to seize her, and drew the bow.

Perhaps her hand shook, as she had resolved that it should not do. Perhaps the spider was too near, and too much above her, for the arrow to find the soft passage that it required. From whatever cause, though it struck the eye at which she had aimed, it only quivered there a moment, and fell back to the ground, having struck bone which it could not pierce.

Had she been confronted by a female spider, her conscious life would not have continued for more than a further minute, for the female palpi have piercing claws, but those which grasped her were meant primarily for the caresses of love. No less deadly for that would be the poison fang to which they would have lifted her screaming, struggling body, had not an axe swung with a stroke which half severed one, so that it loosened its grip.

She had been too intent on the imminent danger to be more than dimly aware of scores of men who ran over the open space from the northern wood. But now she felt the grip of the other palp relax, as the injured monster turned to attack him who had inflicted the wound.

It seized him with the palp from which Jalna had been dropped. High in air, Amek looked into the eightfold vacant stare, and saw the poison fang projecting for his destruction. But the one-handed grip which was all that the wounded spider could use left his arms and his axe free. One desperate stroke hacked off the point of the prong, which then, in his half-held position, did no more than deal his shoulder a bruising blow.

And meanwhile there were a dozen of Amek's men who used their axes below. In the next minute, there was but one of the spider's legs which had not lost at least its lowest joint, or had it too injured to do its part.

Amek found himself dropped to the ground, as the tortured beast, vainly seeking safety in flight, tried to flounder away with a whirling of injured limbs, its body dropped so near to the ground that men found it hard to get beneath it to use their halberds as they had been instructed to do.

Amek turned, panting, to the one he had saved. "Are you greatly hurt?"

She looked at him with grateful, admiring eyes. "No. Thanks to you, I am whole." She picked up the shaft with a shaking hand, while her heart beat so that further words were not easy to say. She thought, "I am shamed, unless I can do better than that."

They looked round on a scene of raging conflict which intensified as more and more of Amek's men came running over the open ground, and attacked the spiders in groups.

Arrows were flying thickly, but too loosely aimed to be of more than chance avail against the bony structures which clothed their foes. But halberds were long enough to be thrust upward to deadly ends, and the axes for which Amek had called were of greater use than poker or knife when applied to the sprawling legs. Having so many, could any spider give heed to the protection of all? Each which was crippled reduced mobility, and made it a simpler matter to avoid the grip of the deadly palpi, while closing in for a further blow.

Relf lay in the midst of this confusion, not yet having strength to rise, and Plera stood over him, poker in hand, with teeth bared, though with eyes which were glazed with fear, for she was one to whom any spider, however small, was a thing to dread, and this was nightmare beyond belief. Yet where Relf was, she would be.

Gleda's voice came to her ear. Gleda had stood back at first, as Amek had urged her to do. But then she thought of the other women whom that inferno contained, and she saw she might help.

Now she was at Plera's side. They saw a spider who looked their way.

Relf said: "Get behind the tree. You will lose your lives with no gain to mine."

Gleda said: "We are two. We shall beat him off," which she did not believe.

Jalna was thirty yards away at this time. The spider was nearly fronting her, though not quite. She saw in what peril her friends were caught. The shaft flew.

The spider stood still. Then it slowly sank, as its legs failed. The arrow had gone into an eye, so that only a few inches showed.

Amek looked at her with more admiration than before which is saying much. He said: "You are both woman and man, and in both exceed."

She gave him a merry look, somewhat aslant. "Equally? But my life is one you have saved. It is yours to judge."

There was an understanding between them, more than the words held. Jalna had a happy pride in what she had done, feeling that it would blur the memory of her failure before.

She looked at the spider who had now collapsed to the ground, and her brows drew to a puzzled frown. Should she tell what she saw, or take the praise of that which she had not done?

There was a moment's doubt, which ended as laughter choked her words. She said: "You may thank me too much for that which I did not do. *I aimed at another eye.*"

So it had been. For the shaft, as was plain to see when it was drawn, could not have flown straight, having been damaged when she had used it before.

But her confidence had returned. "Get me shafts," she said to Amek, as one orders a child. "Get me plenty of shafts, and bring axe men to be my guard; and you shall have more spiders than that. Your name is what? Amek? I have known worse. We will call it our lucky day."

Amek thought: "She does not know who I am, or she acts well. But for acting there is no need. Were I lord of the whole earth, she should be my wife, though she kissed or squirmed."

But there would be little squirming from her.

CHAPTER LII.

ROUT!

THE spiders' strategy was good, but their battle tactics had failed. It had seemed needless to close the way by the river bank. In fact, they had not thought of it at all.

But this neglect had meant that the trapped men had come free, with the slaughter of those who had held them in, and a new force, including most of those who had been landing during the night, were active and exultant upon their rear.

This was not decisive, but it was a disadvantage. Now the spiders found that, while they conquered the river bank, and made further landings very hazardous to attempt during the day, they themselves had a numerous foe separating them from the great inlands from which they came.

Amek marshalled his men on the open ground with a gay heart. They were more than four hundred, well provisioned and as well armed as he could desire. They bore their own dead to the cover of the farther woods, and they left a dozen dead or maimed spiders lying about to show the others what to expect.

They saw movements of spiders over the tree tops, but could not tell whether they were many or few. "Will they come to us, or must we make effort to get to them?" Amek wondered, knowing that he must do the second if they would not oblige him by coming down. For he could not stand idle while his comrades endured the whole fury of their attack.

But he was not left long in doubt of what they would do. They came down, dozens at once. But by then he had withdrawn his men to the farther side of the belt of land they had cleared, with the shelter of the northern woods at their rear (into which Relf had been carried, with some other wounded), where they awaited their rushing foes with a very confident front.

It was at a later hour that Lemno became aware that the battle did not go as well as he would have liked it to do. It had resumed, as his first observation was, with less fury than there had been when the light failed, or, at least, with less numerous foes. For some had been diverted for the attack which was made upon Amek's men, and many had been transferred to capture the river bank.

Now he leaned on a halberd glistening wet with the blood of a spider who sprawled grotesquely among the branches above his head. Slain in the upper boughs, its weight had brought it down lower and lower with noises of snapping wood, until it was now securely wedged between limbs that were too stout to be bent aside. There was a great scythe cut at the rear of its belly, exposing the interior of its spinnerets, from which a stream of green blood still splashed to the ground a few yards from where Lemno stood listening to a report that he did not like.

He said to the man who had brought news that the bank was lost: "Could you swim the river?"

"Yes, lord. I could do that."

"Then get back—not to the place from which you have come, but the nearest part of the bank—that is, due east—from here. Swim to your own land, and tell them not to be faint of heart, nor to cease sending supplies. I suppose the canoes remain?"

"Yes, lord. Except that the spiders destroyed two, which could not be cut loose quickly enough."

"Then they must continue to bring food and arms—and men, who must be told to move at will till a spider appear, which they must fight, and then go on until they find a group This fight will not cease till the last spider is dead. They must continue coming during the night, if the battle should still be on."

He saw the man go, and considered what he should do. The area of conflict was now so large, and its boundaries so vague, that he felt that the sending of messages might be of little avail. He must try to reach the minds of those who would be in need of guidance from him.

But he found that it was not easy to do. Those who were conscious of peril on every side, and enduring exhausting strife, were not tuned to respond to the call of another mind. He tired himself with effort which had little reply.

Then he tried another method. He tried to get into contact with Relf alone, which he soon did.

Relf said that he was still useless for war. He had tried to stand, but dizziness soon had him flat on the ground again. Yet he had his wits. What could he do with them?

He told how matters went around where he lay, as Plera reported. He said that the whole of the open space, as far as Plera could see (they being at the near end, where the first battle was fought) was now a riot. Some men fought on bare ground, with poker, halberd, and scythe. Others lay along the line of the wood, sending shafts where the need was most. It was not won nor lost, but, on the whole, it went well.

Where was Gleda? She should be with him, but had twice ventured out to give help to those who had greatest need. He believed she was with Jalna now. They had combined with some others in a cunning plan by which spiders were lured into a position for Jalna to kill, and three lay dead in a little space, and another had blundered away, carrying death in its head.

Lemno asked that Plera should call together all whom she could, with a request that they would use their wills to augment his; and, with this help, after a time, he was conscious of getting larger response. When it was as much as he could hope, seeing how men were engaged, and that he could not expect to reach the unpracticed minds of those whom Amek had brought, he sent this message abroad: "The spiders have taken the river bank, but no one is to be disheartened by that. The war will go on till it is won. You must all risk death, for, if you do not, you will be certain to die. But the spiders have many dead. Make the dead more. When they fly, as they will tomorrow, if not today, remember that they can run fast for a short time, but not long. They must be pursued till the last is sped. There is one order for all: *Attack the nearest spider you see, and, when it is dead, attack the next beyond that.* If you join in groups of not more than ten, with some bowmen in each, you will do well."

Having received a response to this message which showed that it had entered resolute minds, and having had it relayed to Amek by Relf's assistance, he turned back to what had become a series of separate battles, each of which would go on till a spider died, though, too often, not before it had inflicted the same fate on its boldest foe.

Four hours later, the spiders ran.

The flight began with those at the extreme point of the peninsula, who would have the farthest to go before they could hope to reach a land which would be clear of their human foes.

Scrambling over the swaying tops of the trees, with rapid movements of many flexible legs, leaping gaps at times, or down to the ground to scuttle up the trees at the other side of an open glade, they went blindly north, turning for nothing nor seeking to fight with those who harried them with flying shafts, and an occasional thrust as chance allowed.

As they fled, they were joined by those they passed, so that they became denser as they progressed.

When they reached the limit of the south wood, and looked down on the cleared space on which Amek fought, they had only to cross it to find the safety for which they fled.

It was a test both of apprehension and courage for Amek's men, who might easily have misread the purpose of the multitude which descended upon them. But the spiders made no effort now, even to harm those who were active in barring their way. They were single-minded for flight, and as they passed they took many wounds, and some stayed.

Jalna's arrows decreased their numbers by four, without counting one which she shot under its spinnerets as it was in the air, leaping toward the top of the tree beneath which she lay. She was not destined to know what that shaft had done, but it was not required for her lasting praise.

There was some pursuit, but it was of little avail for that day. It might be true that a spider cannot run fast for more than a short spurt, but when they took to the tree tops, and woods were dense, how could they be quickly pursued? And men were exhausted by lengthened strife. There must be allowance for that.

188

CHAPTER LIII.

A Question of Marriage Rites

AMEK said: "I have chosen my wife. What are the marriage customs you have?"

Gleda laughed. "You mean Jalna? She will think she has come to her right place."

"What do you mean by that?"

"What I say. It is a thing I am glad to hear, for more reasons than one. She will make you a good wife. But you may take one warning from me. If you wish another woman to die, there need be no blood on your hands. Just make her your second wife."

Amek considered this. He said, half-smiling, "I may be contented with her."

"So I think you should. She will be loyal to you; and I should say she can kiss well."

"But that is not what I asked."

"You asked something I do not know. I should say there are none. Lemno slaughtered the one he had, and we put her liver into the pan. It was as simple as that. And it has worked well."

"But I have none to kill."

"She may forgive that! Her own husband—"

"She is not wed!"

"She was. She nursed a sick man who is dead. I am told she was good to him."

"Had she patience for that? It is good to hear. But I still ask."

"I cannot tell more than I have. Lemno will say."

"I have another question to ask. Does she know who you were?"

"Not from me. I should say not at all. I am the woman that Lemno caught for his next meal."

"Then it is well. It is not a king she would wed, but a brother of yours."

"She will do that? I should say you have caught her well. What do we do next?"

"We ask Lemno."

"That is soon done. Here he comes now."

Lemno joined them as she spoke.

Amek said: "I was telling Gleda that I have found a wife in your land."

"It is Jalna," Gleda explained.

Lemno checked himself in what he was near to say. It was true that it was relief to him to hear, but they were words that Amek might have taken amiss. He said: "You have made a good choice. She is as live as an eel. Does she know how great a queen she will be?"

"Not yet."

"Then you have the more cause for content."

"What I am asking is whether there be any customs in your land which she will wish to observe—any manner in which you wed? Gleda says that she does not know."

Lemno laughed at that. "She knows all she need. But I do not say that you should take example from me. I was caught in a strait net."

"It would be a most strait net from which you would not find a way to break free. But I still ask."

"We have no laws. Women do as they will. But we have a custom, beside which laws would be easy to break. Be a contract made, it is shame to break, be it of goods or flesh. Marriage is not a contract which a man or woman will be unable to keep, so it may not be split without shame, unless both consent. If they do, it is their matter, and none is wronged."

"But of the children which may be theirs?"

"There was once provision for that. But, while law prevailed, all were handed to the State at the end of the first year. I tell that which I do not praise. Men do as they will now, and some keep their young in their own walls."

"Then there is nothing for me to do?"

"There is naught but that which concerns yourselves. But I should add that there are records made, which were by compulsion of old, but are still maintained for prudence to use, for it is a matter which should be clear."

"Then I will wed her by the customs of her own land, they being simple or none. And I will give her the feast my own people expect when I return."

"Which can be soon now?"

190

"Not if you will allow a request. I would complete that which is well begun. I would follow those spiders which still live, while they are wounded, frightened, and spent.

"I would follow them even to the great mountains of snow, till the last is dead. You will know no peace at a less price, for they will be certain to breed, and to come again. I should say that cocoons of eggs will be hanging now, in places you have not seen.

"It will be sport for me and the men I lead; while those of yours, who are still of a starved look, and have fought longer than mine, may eat well, and build houses before they are gripped by the colder days."

"And what part has Jalna in this?"

"She will have the part that a wife should. She will come with me. It is a matter for which the spiders should fret. Her shooting is marvel to watch."

Gleda said: "Lemno can shoot well," and was aware of having spoken a fatuous word.

Amek said indifferently: "So a man should be able to do. But she has a skill—!"

"You should tell that to her," Lemno replied. "It is merely true. And she can take praise."

"So I will. With some other things which are of more present concern."

He went off, and found Jalna, who was eating as vigorously as she did most things to which she inclined. He said: "You know that Gleda is sister to me?"

Jalna opened her eyes. "No! But it is the best news that can be. Lemno will be king of this land, and his sister will have the like power—and will have one subject the more than he."

"You think that? Well, you have seen more than I. I would not say you are wrong. Shall you be content if we stay awhile in this land?"

She said: "It is from here I would never move. Let me tell you this. I have a home, having had a husband, though no children were ours. (If you blame me for that, you may find you will be wrong.) It is a good home, to which we could go. But is starvation a price that you will be eager to pay? Let us stay here, and Lemno will give us a good portion of land."

Amek said: "We stay here. For we shall hunt spiders till the last one is dead, and the last egg is a broken shell. Do you shrink for that? If we wed (as we shall, and that before dawn return), you must do my will, whether as woman or queen."

Jalna looked at him with bright eyes, into which a questioning wonder came, though they had been rebellious before. "Queen? Why do you say that?"

"Because I am king in the farther land. Did you not guess?"

"No. But there was a word said which I supposed to be jest, so that it had a meaning which I misdeemed; and when you said that—but did you not say that Gleda was sister to you? How can both things be?"

"Because she would have been queen there, had she not chosen this nearer land, where Lemno and she think to make rule in a new way."

"In a new way? There is nothing new. Lemno told me that."

"New, I should have said, to our times, and to us. But I know little of that. I am content to be king as my fathers were.

"As it saved my life, I must call it a good way. There is a great city in our land which I have not seen."

"There is one in mine which you will be certain to see."

Amek saw that she had a lively mind, which his thoughts must be agile to match. Lemno had said that she was as live as an eel. He thought that her mind leaped like a flea. But he did not regard her as less for that.

Now she was saying: "We shall be warm there, and very secret and hid, though not from a risen moon." He understood that she made plans for the night.

CHAPTER LIV.

CONCERNING LAW IN A NEW LAND

LEMNO said: "Relf tells me that I can have any power I will, and that I betray them if I decline that which I had not sought. It is a new land, and may be led in a new way. But who am I to do that? If I should give a portion of land, clearly bounded, to each who asks, they will be content to leave justice to me, not fearing I shall oppress them with many laws."

Gleda said: "You must decide now. For the first steps should be in the right way."

As they spoke, they sat on a fallen trunk, while axes thudded among the trees.

Men had been eager to build Lemno a house, which it would be comfort to him to have. When he said yes to that, his first decision had to be made. Should it be larger than those which others would be able to have? Should it have wider stairways and higher doors? He had thought not.

He had seen that there might be a larger building required, perhaps for assembly or other purposes. But his home could stand somewhat apart. It should be as those of other men, neither less nor more.

He had found talking to Gleda clarifying to his own mind. It was not (he thought) that she prompted or changed his decisions, but obscure things tended to become plainer when he had discussed them with her.

He knew that his mind was obsessed by his study of savage, incomprehensible times, and it was particularly with them, and most of all with the period of which he had been reading when this interruption came, that she had the gift of simplifying, so that he could recognize the plausibility of previously incredible things.

Even when he had been bewildered by the effort to imagine how a community could submit to an aggregate of laws beyond individual knowledge, and still submissively elect assemblies to make them more, such a condition of existence had become credible, though not sane, when he had talked it over with her.

He had been brought to believe that men could destroy each other in the thousands for the sake of moving vehicles about quickly, and yet be revolted by the idea of using their victims for the only utility which remained. Yet, to the dead children scattered about the roads, could it be any gain that they were not eaten, but thrown away?

Gleda would always answer with careful words, avoiding anything which would indicate what, to him, must have seemed a supernatural acquaintance with that remote and sombre time on which he supposed himself to be the one living authority. Might it not, she suggested, have been the fact that those who were killed or injured were very quickly removed, so that to millions they would be no more than a hearsay tale?—millions who had never seen a child lying about after it had been squashed under a vehicle's wheels? Besides, was it not the fact that they used to discourage people killing each other in that way when they were drunk—sometimes even sentencing them not to continue the sport for a considerable period?

Lemno admitted the shrewdness of her suggestion. He said that it was a feature of that age which gave an aspect of unreality to its grosser facts that they were so elaborately and systematically concealed. It was planned illusion rather than hypocrisy. Millions must have eaten animals all their lives who had never killed one or seen one killed, and would have thought it a most revolting thing to have done.

Gleda agreed to that, inwardly wondering at the thoroughness with which he had reconstructed in his imagination that which had been native to her. She said: "They may have honestly supposed that it showed them to be humane. Human nature is queer."

"Yet at the time with which I was dealing," he answered, "this capacity for self-delusion was threatening the very existence of those who occupied the countries where any semblance of freedom remained—as it did, in a fluctuating way, in some of those law-ridden lands. They knew that an alien tyranny, ruthless and sinister, crept like a black shadow across the earth, and had enslaved more than half of its inhabitants; yet, because it had not directly assaulted their own lives, it appears that millions were less concerned at its growing threat than irritated by the voices of those who warned them. It is a cause of regret to me that I am no longer likely to know the outcome of the world struggle which was imminent in the year to which I had come."

"We may hope to learn that, if we will, from whoever will take over the work you left; but I should say you will be busy with greater things. Let the past go, if we can build better today. And yet—"

She paused, as a memory intruded upon her: the memory of an old Bond Street room, and of what a wizard had said to her.

Lemno looked at her curiously. When they talked of these savage times he always had a strange sense of imminence, as though it were close at hand. He asked: "And yet—what?"

"Only this: that I have been told that past and future are one. That the present is all that is, and it never goes; that time is like the surface of the earth, which is not endless but never ends, as there is no place where it began. It is beyond comprehension. But so the simple fact of the earth's unboundaried surface would be, if the sight of a ball had never come to our eyes, or its idea to our minds."

"You must have been taught," he said, "by those whose thoughts do not keep to the trodden road. They would be a pleasure to meet."

She did not answer that. Turning it aside, she said abruptly: "Do you not intend to use telepathy for common decision, as is done in your old land? Why do you talk as one who must rule in a new way?"

"It is fairly asked. I have asked myself, and have found no simple reply. But of the fact I am sure. There will be many things to be decided quickly: many to plan. There must be clear thought and a single will.

"It may be that our method—which was experiment, nothing more, when the famine came—was only possible in a settled, leisurely time.

"It may also be that it was only possible then to those who had been used to the yoke of law, though they had thrown it aside.

"Yet I shall not reject that method, either for distribution of knowledge or for the securing of common consent. I have no thought to rule, except by willing accord. Nor will I have an array of force, such as has been custom both of tyrannies and of those governments which have professed to have the support of popular will."

Gleda said nothing to that. She had a thought that occasions might come when appeals to force would be inevitable, especially if it should first be tried by others. Could argument with the spiders prevail? Could any treaty be made with them? And were there not men as alien-minded?

He met her silence with words which showed that he was not insensitive to unspoken thought: "You may think that I plan in vain.

195

You may think that changes will surely come. Do you think I am blind to that? Is any permanence possible amid the mutability of all earthly things? Will men remain as they are now, when there are no spiders to fight?

"In the old days of which we have talked, men fought laws, which were stretched everywhere, like the spiders' cords, to entrap their feet. They may have found sport in that. But some sport they must surely have. It will ever be the same, and a new thing. But I am fortunate in the start we shall make, and in having you."

It was a concluding word which would be pleasant for any woman to hear. Should she go back to the old time, and the old life, as she knew she could?

She thought not. She was here. She would see it through.

She gave a laughing reply: "Fortunate? So you are. For you will always be sure of your next meal."

He had no answer to that.

CHAPTER LV.

But Not the End?

SHE was the largest of those who fled. Ruthless, resolute, cool and deadly in all she did.

She was neither young nor old. Twice before, she had woven a silk cocoon to contain her eggs, and had contrived a good place for it to hang. Further eggs (which were too small to be of any inconvenience to her) were now in the central pouch which produced them.

She had much less than a human brain, but there were fewer matters with which it was active to deal. It gave no thought to the Cosmos. It was indifferent to ethics, and to abstractions of every kind. But in the practical matters pertaining to her own existence, and that of her spider kind, she was logical, subtle, and alert.

So far, she had been equal, and more than equal, to all the crises and occasions of life. She had been collected by her mother at birth, with her brothers and sisters, from the cocoon in which she was hatched, and had lived for some weeks on her mother's back, watching all that she did with the blank stare of her eight unwinking eyes; and when she, and her brothers and sisters, had felt equal to independent life, she had led the way, with a sudden leap which had put her before them all, and found safety beneath a stone while four of the weaker or less alert had been prey for her mother's jaws.

That was the law of life to which she had been born, and to which she conformed herself when her own carefully nurtured broods had raced for life before her rapacious and sufficiently successful pursuits.

She had had the three amorous engagements which her three pregnancies had required. Each had meant the acceptance of a lustful but wary and frightened mate, with whom she had had the ritual of dalliance and long embraces appropriate to such occasions; but when emotion had cooled, and there was a cautious loosening of legs, she had never failed in the final bout, which would provide the wedding feast that such a climax should surely have.

There might be female spiders who swoon absurdly with the excitement of copulation to come, so that their mates can drag them away by the leg, make them pregnant in a quiet corner, and walk safely away before they regain their suspended wits.

There might be others who failed to observe their mates' caressing palpi slip silken cords around them, to be tightened at the right time, so that they would be robbed at last of the meal they had hoped to have, being unable to wriggle free before the flight of those who thought more of their own lives than of giving pleasure to them.

There might be females of her own active, rapacious kind who were not always quick enough to seize a retreating mate before the ecstasy of copulation had wholly ceased.

But she had done it all in a better way. Three times she had seized the critical second to grip her mate in an embrace which was not of love; or was, at best, love of a kind which would be no pleasure to him. Three times she had wound the fatal ropes around him, strand by strand till the last of his many legs had lost its freedom to kick wildly about; and three times she had hung a living mate in her larder, to wait the time when she would take him down, and he would be privileged to make a meal for the good of the coming eggs. Through all her life, there had been no failure at all.

And now, in this great battle with invading vermin, she had felt no wound, and four times she had slain a man.

No less for that, she knew that the battle was lost and the fighting done.

Amek's men, working now systematically through the woods, would not be likely to overlook a cocoon of eggs such as she must hang in the right position for them to hatch.

She was well ahead of pursuit when the eggs were laid from the womb which her waist contained, and she spun a cocoon in no haste for those who (if they should live at all) would never sit on a mother's back. But she meant that they should have the best chance of life that her ingenuity could contrive.

They caught her the next day, and a man died before Jalna's arrow went in at a fatal spot; but that was because she had lost time in doubling back, so that the cocoon would be hanged and hidden in a place where it would not be found, it having been searched before.

ABOUT THE AUTHOR

SYDNEY FOWLER WRIGHT (1874-1965) penned over seventy volumes of science fiction, fantasy, classic mysteries, historical novels, poetry, and non-fiction, many of them being published by the Borgo Press Imprint of Wildside Press.

www.ingramcontent.com/pod-product-compliance
Lightning Source LLC
Chambersburg PA
CBHW032007240626
47153CB00003B/1157